Florida,

the Wild Side

Daniel Hance Page

PTP
PTP Book Division
Imprint of Saguaro Books, LLC
Arizona

Copyright © 2023 Daniel Hance Page
Printed in the United States of America
All Rights Reserved

This is a work of fiction. Any names or characters, businesses or places, events or incidents, are fictitious. Any resemblance to actual persons, living or dead, or actual events is purely coincidental. No part of this book may be used or reproduced by any means, graphic, electronic, or mechanical, including photocopying, recording, taping or by any information storage retrieval system without the written permission of the publisher except in the case of brief quotations embodied in articles and reviews.

Reviewers may quote passages for use in periodicals, newspapers, or broadcasts provided credit is given to *Florida, the Wild Side* by Daniel Hance Page and PTP Book Division, an Imprint of Saguaro Books, LLC

PTP Book Division
An Imprint of Saguaro Books, LLC
16845 E. Avenue of the Fountains, Ste.325
Fountain Hills, AZ 85268

ISBN: 9798864103326
Library of Congress Cataloging Number
LCCN: 2023948933
Printed in the United States of America
First Edition

Dedication

Marg, Hank, Jim, Ivadelle, Sheldon, Colleen, Shane and Shannon Page, John, Dan and the Robinson family, Lester and Rose Anderson, Doug, Don, Bob Sephton and families, Garry and the Pratt family, the Massey family, Murray, Sue and the Shearer family, Joe and Linda Hill, Macari Bishara, Joan LeBoeuf, Kevin, Alison and Michaela Griffin, Jerry and Gaye McFarland, Dr. David and June Chambers, "Mac" McCormick, Grant Saunders, Frank Lewis and other friends with whom we have enjoyed the wilderness.

Left to right: Jim Page (Writer's brother), John Robinson (Friend), Dan Robinson (John's son), Dan Page (Writer)

"Gather memories to last forever that you may revisit often when you dream."

Moonstar

"We may not arrive at our port within a calculable period, but we would preserve the true course."

Henry David Thoreau

Other books by Daniel Hance Page

Arizona, the Wild Side
Olympic National Park, the Wild Side
Killbear Park, the Wild Side
Smoky Mountains, the Wild Side
Yellowstone, the Wild Side
Banff, the Wild Side
Return of the Wild
Florida Journeys
Pelican Sea, a Legend of Florida
Walk Upon the Clouds, a Legend of the Rocky Mountains
The Pirate and the Gunfighter
The First Americans and Their Achievements
Life is a Fishing Trip
Riley, the Dog Visitor
Bear Trap Mountain
Where Wilderness Lives
Many Winters Past
The Journey of Jeremiah Hawken
Told by the Ravens
The Maui Traveler
Wilderness Trace
Arrowmaker
Trail of the River
Pelican Moon
Legend of the Uintas

Chapter 1

The Holiday

Present Day

After arriving late at night, Jake Sands, gradually, by dawn's first light saw the room he had rented. Although the place at first stirred little interest, the rush of warm water in the shower cleared away the grayness of fatigue and he started to appreciate his surroundings.

Page

Leaving the room, he stepped into a sunlit morning where a slight breeze, stirring in from the Gulf, carried a fragrance of salt and fish. He walked to his rented car, drove to a coffee shop and purchased two cups of awakener. Returning to the room, he pulled aside all drapes, bringing into view the motel's office along with a path leading into the distance where waves on the Gulf danced in sunshine.

Jake was of medium height and well-muscled, although this strength was almost covered by loosely fitting clothing. Black, yet graying, hair was swept away from his face where there was revealed calm features. Greenish-brown eyes appeared to look out on a world to include the sea.

Florida

He opened windows, allowing the entry of outside air, laced as it was by a slight scent of salt and fish. With the world he sought now present, he sat down on a comfortable chair and welcomed a first sip of what turned out to be richly flavored, strong coffee.

Now, he thought, *the day starts and my holiday begins. I would like to look forward to days of rest yet there is a flaw in the view. A hook on a line has caught me and an invisible yet powerful filament draws me not forward but back. I can't unhook myself regardless of how valiantly I swim against the pull, as a fish too well hooked to be free.*

I got caught in my home's attic on a day when rain pounded outside and kept me indoors where I never stay except when trapped, he recalled. *This should've been the first warning of trouble to come yet such a signpost, as most others was not seen until I look back. I felt the hook when I saw the old, faded photo under glass with an outdated frame.*

In the picture there were two people, a man and woman. They stood at the back of a cabin under a carved, wooden sign proclaiming, Sands Lodge. In neatly printed, inked words beside the two people were the names, Jessica and Feston Sands.

I know from past information, noted Jake, *the two people in the photo are my great grandparents and they lived in Florida. I'm supposed to be on a holiday; however there is no rest when I'm not free but pulled back by invisible, gossamer lines to another time, a different place and two people I've never met yet their lives are haunting me as if they are not the past but the future. If I'm to go on a holiday, I must first seek this future. To do otherwise is to turn away from the trail of my life, as each person's unique journey, marked by signposts. The old photograph is such a marker, being not just an old picture of the past but a sign of my future. I came on this journey to rest. Now the only rest can be obtained by acknowledging why I'm here. This motel is not a destination; it is only a beginning.*

The coffee is now cold, he discovered after trying another sip. *I'll drive again to get a hot drink and this time an accompanying breakfast.*

Jake drove along a causeway bordered by palms with the Gulf on one side and Intracoastal Waterway on the other. *The wilderness of the ocean comes up to the land very noticeably,* observed Jake. *As a result, regardless of how many buildings are constructed here, they are not important compared to the wildness of the sea. The prevalence of water will always supply this region with greatness no inland city can ever match. An almost constant breeze brings freshness even on the hottest days. Water attracts sea birds. Fish bring fishermen. Seafood restaurants are the finest in the country because of the surrounding influence of the Gulf and freshness of food provided. Next to the Intracoastal, a restaurant is in sight. I'll park on the lot next to the docks and hope the menu includes breakfast.*

The restaurant's door was open so Jake walked inside to be greeted by the same freshness of air as it entered through open windows on three sides. He sat at a table providing a view of the docks and water. The surface was calm, only rippled occasionally by fish feeding on floating insects.

Walking to Jake's table and pouring him a cup of coffee, a woman asked, "Coffee?"

"Thank you," he replied.

"Menu?" she asked again.

"No," he said. "Pancakes please and home fries."

"Anything else?" she asked.

"Information," he said.

At the sound of that word, the woman appeared to awaken and see him for the first time. She amply filled out her clothes that were topped by an apron. Her grayish-black hair was cut short. She had apparently given up worrying about appearances years ago and each year had added lines to her face—although some fire continued to flicker in her black eyes. Impressed by the sight of this customer, especially by his eyes, she said, "I have your answer. What is your question?"

"Confidence is good," he noted, smiling.

"Experience gives confidence," she stated.

"Have you heard of the Sands Lodge?" he asked.

"No," she answered. "But with more details I could direct you to someone who would know."

"Somewhere along this coast," he explained, "my great grandparents, Jessica and Feston Sands, built a lodge. I have a faded photo of them standing in front, actually at the back, of their building and that picture has hooked me and brought me here."

"There's a captain who works at the local museum," explained the woman. "By the way, my name is Florence but I'm just called Flo. The captain's name is Caleb Collins. Most people call him Captain or Cap. His life is the sea. He would know the coast and its history. He runs a tour boat here along the Intracoastal and picks up passengers at the dock. You should talk to him and go for one of his tours. You won't be disappointed. I'll tell you when he comes to the dock."

"Thank you," replied Jake. "I like your answer."

"I like your question," she said before walking to a counter and placing the order.

Flo returned with a refill of coffee. Shortly afterward, she brought pancakes and potatoes.

Jake enjoyed the meal then sipped the drink slowly, waiting for the tour boat to appear. Other customers arrived, keeping Flo busy before she called out, "Captain's here. Tour boat is approaching."

She brought the bill and Jake left payment along with a tip at the table. Before leaving, he said to Flo, "Thanks for your help."

"You'll enjoy the journey—even if you don't leave the dock," she replied. "The ride's just an extra."

Stepping outside, being greeted by sunlight and a scent of the sea, Jake walked to the dock's edge to meet the boat. It came to the dock without tapping it, piloted by an obviously experienced guide.

"All aboard," shouted the captain and Jake stepped inside. He sat just before the captain said, "Flo called me and said you were waiting for a tour and you had questions."

The boat reversed and the tour began. The captain had white hair dropping to slightly stooped shoulders. His tanned face seemed to be steered forward by a slim, protruding nose reminiscent of a ship's rudder. Lines on his skin marked chronological age although he had the watery blue eyes of a dreamer who saw not the world as it was now but the way it used to be with high seas and travel to far-off places. By seeing the past, he found more interest than in the present, where the craft he steered was a tour boat and the Intracoastal was always calm. "You a fisherman?" the captain asked Jake.

"Yes," he answered.

"You have a license and extra snook permit?"

"Yes," he replied again.

After removing a fishing pole from a ledge along the boat's side, the captain said, "Bait this line and throw it out toward the mangroves. There are snook around. Shrimp are in that bucket. With only one tourist in the boat we might as well do some fishing."

As directed, Jake sent the baited line out near a border of mangroves. Almost immediately there was a strike. The pole bent from the force of a fish seeking deeper water.

"Beats sittin' on your ass watching docks and houses doesn't it?" asked the captain.

"Fishing's better here than on the charter boats," exclaimed Jake.

"Years at sea puts salt in your veins and water in your eyes," exclaimed the captain. "They are tears for what I now have only to remember rather than direct experience."

"We're not imagining this battle," exclaimed Jake.

"No and your fish is beside the boat," observed the captain before, with the flash of a net, a snook was soon tumbling on board.

"We need one more," directed Caleb with his eyes flashing and a grin lighting up his face.

Again the line went out. A second battle followed, adding another snook to the boat's floor.

Reaching out for the pole, the captain replaced it along with the bucket of shrimp. "We both have a fish for this evening," he noted. "Never take more than we need and the sea will always provide—as with all natural life. Respect we must have and we will be accepted by the wild."

"More can be learned from you during one tour than many people teach during many trips," said Jake. "When the seas you remember become calm, I want to ask you a question."

"Asking questions?" mused Caleb. "We don't have to ask questions. To get answers we only have to start doing what we want to learn. When I was younger, I asked an old guy with whom I worked, if he would show me how to paddle a canoe as he did. He replied the only way to learn how to paddle a canoe was to paddle a canoe—so I did; learned how to sail the same way. I went to the old school of hard knocks. In that school, you don't have to be told twice."

"Guess I'd better not ask any questions," observed Jake, smiling.

"Go ahead," offered Caleb. "I've already answered but I don't mind following up if I can be of further help."

"My great grandparents were Jessica and Feston Sands," explained Jake. "They started a lodge somewhere around this area on the coast of the Gulf. The place was called Sands Lodge. I'm trying to find it."

"Earliest lodges in this area were farther south where shores were sandy and good for swimming," recalled Caleb. "If you drive south fifty miles and look around, you will find the lodge if any trail remains. Sometimes the sea keeps secrets. More is secret than what has been recorded—and there are always surprises. The rising sun will often shine for you on moments of happiness that, in your later years, you can look back on to collect memories you cherish. I take such journeys all the time—especially when there are no other people around and it's just me with the sound of water splashing against the bow of my boat. That's a pure sound I've heard no other way in any other place. Just the Gulf and I; and it'll never let you down although seas get high. When a person is angry, stay away. When the sea is angry stay in port. Trouble only comes when we can't stay away or in port."

"You charge admission but you can never be paid for what you provide," noted Jake.

"I've given only what you're able to see and hear," he replied. "When you got on the boat, I saw someone with whom I could ride the seas. Many people park their asses down and seem to be sitting more on their minds than butts. Such folks get nothing for the cost of admission and I receive no joy in their lack of view. They are really staying home—although they change locations and call their trips vacations."

Sunlight sparkled on the water, but the day had a light that was not just sunshine. Looking toward the mangroves, yet seeing only the past, Caleb said, "I went to sea and I've never left it nor has it left me. Drive farther south and you will find your lodge if it is to be found. If other trails don't take you where you want to go, there's a person who might be able to help you. His name is Roger Tomkins. He used to work with me at the museum. Some people think he became a hermit but he didn't. He's just reclaiming the peace and quiet he missed in life. He traveled the backcountry until he found the foundation of a cabin. He rebuilt the place and lives there now. He might know about Sands Lodge. We are getting close to the dock. Before we go to shore, I'm going to draw a map, showing where we are and the way to find the cabin. You might want to stay at the Gulf Breeze Resort. Roger stays there when he visits the Gulf."

"Enjoyed your company," said Jake as he carried one fish and stepped out of the tour boat. "And thanks for the map."

"I enjoyed meeting you," replied Caleb. "You too are a captain. We know each other when we meet—and travel the seas—always to far places although the actual distance covered might be short."

After putting the boat into reverse, he said, "Flo was right."

Jake carried the snook to his car. He opened the trunk and dropped the catch onto a spread-open newspaper. Back at the room, he filleted the fish. After putting unusable remnants into a trash bin he carried other pieces to the water's edge where he fed a cloud of gulls.

Having looked after food considerations, he went for a walk. Waves were cresting before sending sheets of bubbling water across the sand. Jake walked through these moving flows and entered the world of the sea. He relaxed while listening to sounds of waves accompanied by calls of birds.

He approached a woman just as she pulled back on a fishing pole. It bent and jumped in response to thrusts of a struggling fish. Being hauled up onto the sand, the fish's silver sides flashed in sunlight as the woman said, "I've caught a mackerel—and a good one."

"Great catch," said Jake. "Takes a good fisherman to catch an exceptional fish."

"Most fish are caught by the smallest number of fishermen," replied the woman, "and dinner is the reward."

"With two of us here, I wonder how many others aren't catching anything," added Jake.

"Most of them," she said, unhooking the mackerel. "This is a wonderful day."

Reminded of a fine meal waiting, Jake walked back to the room. He found sufficient supplies present in cupboards to cook the fillets after coating them with corn meal.

The meat was white and the finest quality. Following the meal, he cleaned the kitchen then walked to the office to mention he would be leaving in the morning.

With his bill paid, he sat on a chair in front of the motel. Sipping beer, he watched the sunset gather colors from the sky, leaving behind hues of night.

A rising moon painted a silver path from the horizon to the shore where a night heron hunted for fish. The egrets had returned inland while the great blue heron rested on the motel's roof.

First rays of morning sunlight flashing across the landscape found Jake Sands driving southward. Holding a cup of just purchased coffee, he welcomed a new day.

I'll ask people about the lodge, he resolved. *If no leads appear, I'll use the map to visit the guy at the cabin.*

When he came to a region scattered with lodges, he rented a room at the Gulf Breeze Resort then decided to save the rest of the day by chartering a boat to go fishing. *Captains who know the water*, he concluded, *might remember the location of the Sands Lodge.*

Fishing boats were tied up at the dock, a sign of a slow day in the charter business. He approached the only person present, as he was hosing down his boat.

"Do you have time for some fishing?" Jake asked this captain who was of medium height and somewhat nondescript except for a seemingly perpetual frown, as if he were always seeing problems. Rather than sporting an actual beard, he just appeared to have not bothered shaving for a long time. A soiled hat topped his head, shading dark eyes.

"There's time left in the day, particularly since nothing has happened until you arrived," he answered. "Get aboard. We don't want to waste the time we have. Rates will be for half a day. What kind of fish are you after?"

"Some good fillets for tonight's meal," Jake replied before paying and tipping the man.

"That makes the choice easy," noted the guy. "I'm Sam Wilson."

"Jake Sands," said Jake.

"My wife wants some drum scales," explained Sam. "She uses them to represent flower petals in her shell pictures. I could get what she wants and fillets for you."

"Drum will be our fish," declared Jake, before the boat was untied and motor started.

The water was calm and starting to reflect colors from the evening sky where the sun was descending into a purple haze along the horizon. Into these colors, the boat sliced at full speed. Buildings were left behind, replaced by a shoreline of mangroves. Cormorants and egrets started to find places on branches in preparation for approaching night.

After stopping the boat in a bay, Sam said, "I'll bait two lines, one for each side of the boat. This is a good place to catch red drum. Let your line move for a while before setting the hook."

Lines were set. The men waited while birds kept arriving, increasingly decorating mangroves with touches of black and white. Colors of sky and water darkened.

Jake enjoyed the evening's calm with gathering birds and deepening hues. Bringing his attention back to his line, he was surprised to see it moving sideways.

He waited then set the hook. The pole came alive and bent as Jake discovered he could not immediately turn the fish. It swam toward the other line as it started to move. Sam set the hook just before the lines crossed, doubling the weight of fighting fish.

"I thought I'd seen it all," shouted the captain. "I have no luck usually. The wilderness must like you."

Pulling together, the two lines slowly brought the catches to the boat where both men used nets to bring the fish aboard. "Never seen this before," exclaimed Sam. "That enough fillets for you."

"I only want some for tonight's meal," he answered. "Your wife will have scales and fillets."

"Never have seen such a thing," muttered Sam, before starting the motor.

Having to shout over the sound of the motor, Jake explained, "My great grandparents had a lodge somewhere around here. They were Jessica and Feston Sands. Their lodge was called Sands Lodge. Have you ever heard of them? Do you know where the lodge might be located?"

"Have never heard of them or their lodge," answered the captain.

Back at the dock, when Sam was filleting the fish and saving scales, he proclaimed, "I've never seen such luck. It must belong to you because it isn't mine."

While he worked, pelicans scrambled for chunks of fish thrown into the water while a snowy egret stood on the filleting table and started to pick up small remnant pieces.

Sam flashed the side of his knife at the bird. It stayed clear of the thrust then returned to stand and watch for food. The knife flashed again and the egret flew into the crimson sky, soon becoming lost from view.

On the table, there remained the bird's severed toe. The knife flashed again, knocking the incongruous piece of foot into the water.

"You have to have respect," Jake told the captain. The glare in Sam's eyes told Jake all he needed for the man's reply. Jake was given a piece of fillet in a clear, plastic bag.

He took the package, saying, "Your wife will be pleased with this fishing trip.

"Yes, she will be pleased," the man answered.

Jake walked to his car. Murkiness had started, beginning the night. He drove to his rented room where he withdrew two cans of beer from the refrigerator. Carrying them, he sat on a chair providing a view of the Gulf where waves splashed against the shore. This song of the sea rested his mind while he sipped the drinks and relaxed. An almost constant companion of a breeze rustled palm leaves. *Tomorrow*, he resolved, *I'll try to find Roger Tomkins' cabin, the hermit who isn't a hermit.*

The manager of the resort, Eileen Thomas, left her office and was about to go for a walk when she saw Jake. After she sat beside him, he gave her a can of beer, saying, "I was expecting you."

"Sure you were," she replied, laughing. She was young and slim with black hair, brown eyes and apparently the strength needed to cope with challenges of running a resort. "I spend too much time looking after eccentric people and often forget to come out and enjoy the Gulf."

Standing, she said, "I'll be right back." When she returned, she carried a paper bag filled with more beer. Giving a can to Jake, she asked, "Ready for a walk?"

They strolled beside cresting and breaking waves outlining a trail into night where nothing else of the world could be seen except for the sky lit by stars and a rising moon. There were only words spoken by two people who found companionship in being, even for a short time, together in a realm where they seemed to be all there was. Each series of words, with thoughts they expressed, were exchanged with highest clarity resulting in Jake and Eileen connecting to a depth far beyond what could be expected to form in the short time they were together. As each person found a friend, neither one nor the other thought of stopping. They walked until tired then returned in bright moonlight.

Before entering the office, she said, "In the ocean, there are shallow places and deep. Although we have known each other only for a short time, we have met deeply. I enjoy these moments. Looking back, they are what we remember. Peace and quiet provides an opportunity for such events to occur. Another man comes here who seeks such journeys. People have called him a hermit but he isn't one. He is a person who decided to get away from life's routines and through peace and quiet visit deep places in an attempt to better understand and enjoy life."

"You sound as if you're talking about a person I'm going to visit tomorrow," observed Jake. "He is Roger Tomkins."

"That's the one," she exclaimed. "He stays here occasionally to enjoy the Gulf."

"I've heard of him twice although I haven't actually met him," declared Jake.

"There's no such thing as coincidence," she whispered, before entering the office.

Returning to his room, Jake prepared a meal of drum fillets then welcomed sleep.

In the morning, holding the usual cup of coffee, he started driving while following a map drawn by Caleb Collins.

Turning off paved roads, Jake came to one of sand. He followed it and, after crossing a stream, he recognized a two-lane route marked on the map.

I hope this ends well, Jake thought while he proceeded into a wilderness where foliage was not only on both sides but also overhead. *This route is as a tunnel into a world of trees, foliage and vines,* observed Jake. *Visual beauty is matched by stirring melodies of bird songs. I'm relieved to see there are a few places where a vehicle could pull off the lane to let a second vehicle pass if it were approaching from the opposite direction. Backing up could be hazardous.*

Increased sunlight reaching the ground indicated a clearing ahead just as Jake saw a cabin. Back of it there was an extensive garden.

In a shaded area, a man was butchering a boar. "Welcome to a new day," shouted the man, after Jake parked and stepped out of his car. "If you're staying for a meal," continued the man, "we're having roast boar from the garden. I grow vegetables. When wild pigs root around in my small crop, the garden also provides meat to roast."

The guy wielded a knife as a person who conserves energy, making each slice produce desired results. His medium length hair was white as was his beard, leaving little room for a well-tanned face where gray eyes flashed. "I'm Roger Tomkins," he said.

"A friend of yours, Captain Caleb Collins, suggested that I visit you," said Jake. "I'm Jake Sands."

"If Caleb sent you here, you are welcome," said Roger. "I worked with him at the museum. He is as fine a person as one could ever find with whom to sail the seas in actual experience or down memory lane. I go and see him occasionally as I also visit Eileen Thomas, manager of a resort beside the Gulf."

"I enjoyed meeting both of them," replied Jake.

"They probably told you some details of how I looked back at my life and decided time had come to alter course before my sailing was over. If I had to do my life over again I would try to enjoy it more, seeing the journey as an opportunity rather than an ordeal, placing one day after the other until my hair and beard were both white.

"I thought I would also seek out more peace and quiet that I'd often missed in the din and roar of one thing after another without stopping at an island and asking for some understanding of the journey and the course I was taking. So I sought out a quiet place, checking all over until I discovered a foundation indicating a home had been here previously. I rebuilt the home. Afterward, I found the long lost peace and quiet but I continue to check in with the outside world.

"Maybe enough has been said about me. Thoreau said, 'I should not talk so much about myself if there was anybody else whom I knew so well.' I have a tendency to talk too much when I have someone with whom to share words. I'd like to hear from you.

"I'm going to prepare roast pork for a meal. While you are waiting you can sit on one of the chairs under the live oak and I'll bring out some beer."

"Thank you," replied Jake, before walking toward the chairs. He was sitting when Roger brought the beer. Working quickly, he soon had boar meat roasting on a spit over a fire. As the meat cooked, Roger sat, welcoming shade while he and Jake sipped cold drinks.

"I came here because of a photograph I found in a box of notes in my attic," explained Jake. "The old photo showed a man and woman standing at the back of a building with a sign overhead identifying the place as Sands Lodge. The two people were Jessica and Feston Sands, my great grandparents. The picture hooked me and has pulled me south on a journey to find this lodge. I have stayed in various places, talking to people until messages led here."

"You have compared yourself to a fish getting hooked and pulled," noted Roger. "Well you've just been netted. After finding this foundation, I asked people in the area if they had any records about early settlers. I discovered that the people who built this foundation for their cabin were Jessica and Feston Sands. There is a trail leading from here to the Gulf. Feston and Jessica moved from this site and built a lodge beside the Gulf. Behind the lodge there is an inlet where a stream enters. This water has to be crossed to get to the beach. As I said, there's a trail going from here to the site of the lodge. At the inlet I have left a canoe. The widest section of the inlet can be crossed with the water coming up to a person's chest. I think I might be the only one who has found the site where the lodge was located. Likely I'm the first one who has looked for it. There's nothing left of the buildings but a foundation. It isn't hard to find for anyone who's actually looking for it. To get there, you could just follow my trail. I've marked the route with trail tape. Many people take the path in both directions. I meet these travelers all the time and I enjoy the company. Mainly the hikers are adventurers or photographers. Around this neck o' the woods people tell visitors if you want to see old Florida or the Florida backcountry take the journey to Roger Tomkins' cabin."

"That's great news," exclaimed Jake. "Thank you Roger. All I have to do now is walk to the lodge's foundation and I will have entered the snapshot of time caught by the photograph."

"The trail is well marked and easy to follow," observed Roger. "People take it all the time. Regardless of how well marked the route is a person should not enter wilderness unless he or she is prepared with necessary knowledge and supplies."

"I have a back pack filled with equipment and required items," confirmed Jake.

"I'm going to add a gift from your great grandparents," added Roger before he entered his cabin. When he returned, he carried a bag of oranges. With a second visit to the cabin, he brought items for a meal of roast pork. "Jessica and Feston planted orange seeds throughout this region," he explained. "These seeds have given us lots of orange trees. Oranges will supply you with water and nourishment for hiking the trail."

"Thank you," said Jake. "We both appreciate their gifts."

"Now I'm going to serve you a meal of roast boar fresh out of the garden," proclaimed Roger, before he started arranging plates and topping them with food.

While both men savored the tender and flavorful meat, Roger explained, "Pork should always be well cooked. If some types of meat are not sufficiently cooked, they can be harmful to people. A few years ago a guy shot a bear. The meat was not well grilled and the guy ended up in a wheel chair."

"This food was superbly roasted," added Jake.

"I'll package some pork for your hike—and the oranges," offered Roger.

"You have been a wonderful help," observed Jake.

"I've enjoyed the story of Jessica and Feston," said Roger. "Maybe someday I'll be telling stories with the account of Jake Sands."

"Hope it isn't at a grave marker where you're telling the stories," countered Jake.

"Yours wouldn't be the first—nor the last," added Roger.

"I'm in no hurry for that," said Jake. "I won't take a marker with me."

"I'll start making one," joked Roger.

"Before the marker goes up, I have things to do," said Jake.

He walked to his car and removed a backpack. To it he tied a folded tarpaulin, sleeping bag and tent. On an extra belt, he attached a hatchet and knife, both in leather holders. Lastly, he secured a water bottle. He picked up this equipment, including a walking stick then returned to the shade. After sitting again, he picked up the beer can. "I appreciate your help and information," he said to Roger.

"Sorry to add to the weight you carry but I've prepared a pack with oranges and cooked pork along with boiled potatoes," noted Roger. "A person should never visit wilderness or start any journey without first making careful preparations—and you are careful. Along with food, I put in some beer."

"I'll have to think of some way to help you," exclaimed Jake.

"Don't make me prepare a marker," joked Roger.

"OK," laughed Jake. "Be a pleasure. Hospitality keeps holding me here but I should get traveling."

"I'll show you the start of the trail," offered Roger. "First let's finish the beer—to make one less can to carry."

"Good idea," answered Jake. He rested, gathering strength. Lastly, he attached the equipment and walked with Roger to the trail.

"The route is a natural path between here and the Gulf," explained Roger. "You'll probably meet other hikers as the trail is popular. You'll also come upon some orange trees planted by your ancestors."

"Thanks Roger," said Jake. "The past awaits."

Jake started walking. He was uplifted by the joy of getting started. *All because of a photograph*, he recalled. *That picture of Jessica and Feston Sands brought me to this place—and to what? Their lives were here. They came for their own reasons. Life seems at times to be only a wisp of a breeze often leaving no trace behind. So what is the purpose of it all? We must go through with it to improve ourselves by enduring what we can only experience here. That must be it.*

The route is easy to follow, observed Jake. *The farther I walk the wilder the terrain gets. Birds seem to be always singing. People often take for granted the most important aspects of life—such as a bird's song. I hear these songs less often all the time. Even in my lifetime, I've noticed a drastic reduction in the number of birds. I listen to them more now because these songs are becoming unusual.*

Having pushed onward as far as possible without resting he eventually stopped to sit on the trunk of a fallen tree at the edge of a swamp. Slithering along the water there was a cottonmouth. Some ridges stirred the surface before an alligator struck and the snake vanished in closing jaws.

I'm pleased I packed a hammock, noted Jake. *I wouldn't want to sleep on the ground.*

He resumed traveling until shadows increased, reminding him of the time to prepare a camp. He stretched the hammock between two trees. Up off the ground he also tied the rest of his equipment particularly food. With a sleeping bag in the hammock and tarp above, preparations led to the starting of a small fire. He heated a chunk of pork for the first part of a meal followed by a flavorful and thirst-quenching orange.

While waiting in the hammock for sleep to come, he thought, *nighttime seems to bring all creatures closer until they are right in camp. Croaking of frogs is constant along with splashes. Screams occur occasionally. The snarl of a panther is unmistakable.*

Jake was pleased to have light return, bringing the morning. Without preparing a meal other than savoring an orange, he resumed traveling.

I forgot to ask Roger how much time would be needed to reach the Gulf, recalled Jake. *Roger liked my preparations so there must be a notable distance involved. The trail is so well marked I don't have to worry about staying on the route. I must not get complacent.*

Jake's thoughts returned to the photograph and how it had pulled him to his present location. *The picture,* he recalled, *has taken me back to the lives of Jessica and Feston Sands. Possibly my own life has led me to them. Maybe I've been the same as Roger who said he previously just went from one day to the next without trying to enjoy life or see it as an opportunity. As he once was, I too have been. Do we only think about what we are missing when we are older and look back? This trip has awakened me. I almost feel alarmed.*

Concerned about his recollections, Jake stopped. He looked around. Having seen his life in a new way, he now looked at the trail in a different manner. He could not see it. "Oh wow!" he exclaimed. "What have I done?"

In an attempt to dispel a flicker of panic, he hurried back to find something that looked familiar—like a marker. None appeared.

He stopped. *I went back along the trail of my own life,* he thought, *and forgot to follow the route I was traveling marked by tapes. That was such a huge mistake to make so quickly. Ease of following the path caused me to lose it. I often think of one thing while doing another. That habit has brought me into the Florida wilderness without any idea of where the trail is located. I must think before I pile on more mistakes.*

I did not carry a compass because I know the basic directions with the sun rising in the east and setting to the west. The Gulf is southward. I'll walk to the south.

The journey continued—for days. Each day appeared grayer than the one before it. Food and oranges, first rationed, became scarce. The only aspect increasing was despair.

At night, sounds seemed to be getting louder and coming closer as if they were right around the hammock. Sleeping became more difficult to the point of hardly occurring or at least not remembered.

Walking southward became less and less possible because any attempt at a direct route stopped at a swamp or river. Jake's strength decreased with the shortage of food and orange juice. Roasted frog legs became a main meal. Orange juice was replaced by boiled water. Enjoyments such as coffee stopped even being memories.

After many days and nights, Jake realized he had become focused on death. Compensating for his vanished optimism, he kept traveling more out of habit than any sense of purpose. Each night was repeated as the one before it. Days became indistinguishable one from another. Except for an increasing feeling he was walking toward death, little changed.

One day brought an improvement in the food supply when he threw his walking stick, like a spear, into a rising flock of ibises, bringing down two birds. They were roasted on a spit over a fire and savored ravenously. There resumed a diet of frog legs, boiled water and despair.

Tired, weak and facing death, he stopped, looked around at the surrounding wilderness, and asked, "How could I not see it? I was thinking of death when there is life all around me. Life, the answer, is so obvious yet for so long I did not see it. I was thinking about death with life surrounding me. The wilderness is a messenger, guiding people toward life. That's what Christ is, as is some other prophets, a guide toward life—spiritual life. The wilderness is a messenger guiding toward life—the Creator. I don't need a trail to home. I now see the way. I'm already home."

Jake welcomed the trees, foliage and all other parts of his surroundings he could now view in a new light—the spiritual presence of the Creator. "I feel such a wave of relief now that I've decided to follow the messenger of the wilderness home," he whispered. "I no longer feel like I've been left alone. I now realize I'm part of life beyond myself—of the wilderness—the messenger and connection with the Creator."

How does this happen? Jake wondered. *I stopped turning away, started choosing life and now I see another person.*

Jake approached a man who was sitting and resting his back against a tree. "Welcome," said the man.

"Why are you here?" asked Jake.

"I saw you with the choice you had to make—like every other person," he answered. "You recognized the messenger and chose to stay with the Creator. That's all anyone has to do. I'll show you the other trail." Giving Jake a pack, the man said, "These supplies will help you to enjoy your journey."

"You have thought of everything," exclaimed Jake, placing he extra pack on his back. "Thank you." He followed the man until they came to a tape marking the route to the Gulf. Farther along this path, there was an orange tree. Jake rushed toward it. With shaking fingers, he picked an orange, peeled it and felt a burst of relief when he tasted the delicious juice.

He turned to thank the stranger. Yet the person had vanished. After looking around in all directions, Jake concluded, *the helper is part of my new awareness. He brought me back to the trail. First I'll rest, get energized with oranges then continue traveling to the Gulf.*

He resumed walking until he came to the edge of a river. He attached a large fly to the hook on his fish line then tossed the bait into the stream. In a short time, he pulled a large catfish to the bank.

Setting up camp, he soon had a fire burning. Above it, he roasted the catfish on a skewer. The soft, moist meat along with orange juice helped to restore his strength. Next he savored the pure joy of resting for the first time since before he got lost. *There is no rest*, he resolved, *when I'm worried. Now the pieces of life are back in order and I can find enjoyment in life—just being alive with all the beauty I now see, hear and look forward to in the future. I can make plans and dream again. Seeing the wilderness differently, accurately, for the first time, I've lost any desire to leave it.* When night arrived and found him in the hammock, he experienced again the healing power of deep sleep.

"I'm home," he shouted one morning when, in dawn's first light, he left the hammock after a great night's sleep. "This is my Florida home. Whether people know it or not, when they travel to Florida, or have always been here, they are drawn to home—the natural place. For some, it's the weather or a park. The truest home, with limitless complexities to match interest, is the wilderness—the messenger. People for countless years have known this aspect of the wild. I now see it and have lost any interest in leaving. I have discovered what Jessica and Feston found in Florida. Their cabin and lodge were just shelters or camps. I'm going to establish a more elaborate place to stay for an extended time."

As a first step, he resolved, *I'm going to get clean.* After heating water in a pot, he struggled through the process of shaving away a beginning beard. To complete this aspect he trimmed his hair. For the next process, he removed all his clothes. After washing them, he stretched them out to dry beside the fire. Lastly, he worked on his own scrubbing, getting covered in soapsuds. Using the pot, he kept scooping water from the river and sending down to the ground flows much like enjoying a shower. He dumped the last bucket, opened his eyes and saw a woman hiker staring at him. She wore the finest hiking clothes, had a pack on her back and carried a walking stick.

Surprised and pleased to see her, Jake shouted, "Hi. Would you stay for a meal?"

"Thank you but I can't," she answered. "I'm in a hurry. People are waiting for me." She rushed onward, soon moving out of view along the trail.

Sorry she didn't stay, reflected Jake. *I guess if I had some clothes on she would have been less worried.*

Checking the clothes and finding them to be dry, he put them on before he sat and opened the first of his two cans of beer. "Time to celebrate," he declared before taking a sip of almost warm drink. *Quite pleasant without being chilled*, he noted. *The woman ran away from me but I can celebrate a new beginning with the wilderness—a friend who won't leave me as I had previously tried to run from it. The wilderness is a friend and above all a messenger. From now on, I'll always be walking in the right direction. Night is approaching. I've started to enjoy sleeping again. I'm in my new life. I look forward to getting up in the morning.*

Dawn the next day was greeted with the sounds of perking coffee. Filled with a renewed interest in cooking, Jake prepared pancakes from the backpack the stranger had supplied.

With all preparations completed, he sat to enjoy a plate topped by flapjacks accompanied by an orange. Following the meal, he washed the dishes and repacked them. Lastly he sat while he held a cup of coffee. A wisp of steam curled upward from the cup Jake used to warm his hands before enjoying the first sip.

I've often seen wilderness, he reflected. *Now, for the first time, I understand it. I enjoy such company and am now at home. I have lost all desire to leave yet I'm short of supplies and should return to the car and get restocked. First though, I'll try to find the foundation, a remnant of Sands Lodge.*

Again Jake started following the trail. *The route is well marked along with being a natural part of the land*, he observed. *I'll have to remember to not get careless.*

As he walked, he enjoyed a new sense of companionship with the landscape, appreciating the new vista opening up at each step or turn. Suddenly, before him was the inlet.

I've come to the water, he exclaimed. *There's no canoe. I'll have to find the wide area where the inlet is comparatively shallow.* Walking again, he reached the widening in the stream. He removed his clothes, except for underwear to not shock other hikers. Holding clothes and supplies above the surface, he stepped forward. Water kept rising but leveled off at chest height.

Reaching the opposite side, he looked downstream and was surprised to see the woman he had met previously. She was paddling the canoe across the inlet and approaching the trail.

Jake called out and waved to the other hiker, although there was no response. *Unfortunately,* he thought, *the only other person out here at this time wants to avoid me. I guess first impressions sometimes really are lasting.*

Fully clothed again, he walked to the Gulf. It presented a new world. Whereas the land trail was like a tunnel through foliage, the Gulf was wide open. Water and sky joined at the horizon in seemingly endless vistas where waves moved and birds soared.

I'm now everywhere at home in the countryside or wilderness of the sea, reflected Jake. *The sea, with winding shoreline and endless sky, calls me in a way I particularly enjoy. I must find a place where I can camp.*

He set up the hammock between trunks of sea grapes where there was some shelter from the seemingly constant breeze. After the camp was prepared with its basic comforts, Jake resolved, *everything is ready for a fish dinner.*

Carrying the fish line and walking stick to the water, he followed the shore until he saw a school of scaled sardines or greenbacks. He threw the stick, like a spear, and struck two of the minnows. Catching them, he put one on the hook.

After stripping down to his underwear, he waded out into the salty water. At a suitable depth, he threw the line out as far as possible then released line as he returned to shore. Resting beside his clothes, he waited.

A photograph in my attic hooked me and pulled me here, he recalled. *I enjoy this place and feel its companionship—as the wilderness where the trail is located. Pelicans soar above the waves. Higher, a frigate bird seems to rest in the sky. There are sandpipers checking for food as waves send flows of water pouring onto the sandy shore then back. Ibises also search the shoreline for food. I have just been joined by a great blue heron and a snowy egret. I'll share food with them.*

Something hit the line and Jake excitedly pulled to shore a long, slender ladyfish. He cut small pieces for the egret then gave the remainder to the heron.

With the second minnow on the hook, Jake waded out, threw the line and before he returned to shore a battle started. He stepped out of the water, bringing to shore a large, king mackerel.

He filleted the fish, sharing with his companions before taking to camp two remaining slabs of fillet. They filled the pan and cooked quickly, providing an extraordinary meal. He savored it fully.

Basking in a glow of contentment, Jake opened the last can of beer. *This place is the home I seek*, he concluded. *I'll try to buy this land and build a cabin on the foundation of Jessica and Feston's lodge, the Sands Lodge—my Florida home.*

In the morning, after coffee, Jake started searching among palms, sea grapes, and pines where maybe there once was a lodge. *High water and wind would constantly reshape contours of sand even back from the shore*, he reasoned. Having investigated a long strip of sand, he started checking farther back where trees were more numerous, an indication of shelter from wind or water.

He walked, enjoying the companionship of sky, water and trees until he almost stumbled over the side of protruding mortar. "I can't believe it," he shouted. "No one would see this if he or she wasn't searching for it. I've found the foundation of Sands Lodge."

Chapter 2

The Timucuans

1550

The first light of each new day was greeted by the Timucuan leader, Stone Bear, who sat on the shore, sipped hot, charred corn drink from his wife's pottery cup, and welcomed the day's beginning that could be glorious with colors appearing in the east. From the midst of color, golden light flashed upon the sea finding it to be sending waves to shore.

Increased warmth also flowed with this light as the sky brightened and spirit of life stirred.

The Timucuan people had maintained one of their villages for as long as could be remembered on the long stretch of land bordered by the sea on one side and the mouth of a fresh water stream on the other. This flow of fresh water brought life to crops stretching out from both banks. Numerous bridges crossed the stream above fishponds adding to a stable food supply for the people.

In the village between the stream and sea, Stone Bear had become an important leader with records of exploits tattooed on his skin. People of his village recognized his power. They also knew the source of this power and respected him more for it. Before seeking his work in life he first had sought the maker of it. He had come to the shore each day, watching his surroundings until he understood them. Such understanding gave him strength others saw.

He had watched sea and sky brightening with first light as the sun climbed the sky bringing each new day. Pelicans skimmed above waves, watching for fish as other birds did. All parts of life moved in golden rays while Stone Bear observed them all. All of a sudden, it happened. The scene before his gaze had jumped closer until he entered it—realizing he was part of what he saw while he, as so many others, were connected by the spirit of and in life—the Creator. From the shore that day, he had walked away but he knew the spirit connecting all life was in him as with other people, birds, animals, fish and plants. The source of Stone Bear's strength was in his awareness of the spirit of life.

His life had not become as wondrous as his knowledge of the spirit because much of the world did not have or seek awareness of the Creator. Much of the world had turned away and this brought trouble in many forms.

Stone Bear knew items are supplied and could be taken for food. If there was gathering respectfully, never taking more than was needed or supplied then collection of food was part of life. There was no death, he knew, because life just goes back to the spirit world.

He threw his net and caught small fish. He put one on a bone hook before paddling his dugout out to deep water where he set the line. Afterward, he waited.

His friend, the pelican, swooped in and took the usual place at the back of the canoe. Stone Bear threw his friend small fish.

After the first hit on the bait, Stone Bear waited. The pelican stirred, seeming to know and expect action. The wait was short. A great silver fish jumped completely out of the water. Sunlight flashed on silver sides before the large fish returned to the sea. The canoe, with bird and man, followed the hidden but swimming fish.

The sun climbed the sky. Other pelicans soared past. A frigate bird seemed to wait and watch from the sky where a few clouds drifted.

When the sun was directly overhead, Stone Bear tugged on the line and turned the great fish. More slowly than the first half of the journey, the canoe started to travel back toward smoke on shore where Stone Bear's wife, called White Bird, but usually just Bird, waited. Beside a fire, she had a drying rack along with roasting sticks. Other people accompanied her.

When the silver fish was pulled to shore, many people carried food back to the village. Remaining meat was smoked on a drying rack while some was roasted. The pelican and other birds had been so well fed they returned to the world of birds. The pelican climbed the sky and joined others soaring among clouds, all so noticeably connected for those who wanted to see.

"I was lucky to marry you," said White Bird to her husband while they dined on roasted fish along with potatoes and corn. Her long, black hair shone with oil from seeds. Her face was beautiful, particularly her dark eyes that, when caught in sunlight, were actually brown.

"I feel the same way about you," replied Stone Bear. As others, he kept his hair knotted above his head with a border dropping down to his face where strength showed in his features. In his eyes and manner, there was a central spirit of calmness. This strength, coming from seeing beyond to the spiritual world, drew people to him. They often sought his advice. "Your corn soup is delicious," he added.

A lot of other people will be enjoying fish today," she observed. "Your helpfulness to others adds to the taste of this food."

"There is enough food for everyone," he agreed. "We don't need trouble to get food. There is sufficient supply. Some people seem to want extra. They want what others have. So we have to defend ourselves."

"You are speaking of our new enemies," she stated.

"Particularly our new enemies," he confirmed while he looked out to sea trying to comprehend people who were not like him.

"The Spaniards have come," said Bird. "If they would only leave this land as they found it. The first to arrive called our country La Florida—Land of Flowers.

"At first the newcomers were welcomed to these shores. The welcoming was met with killing on a scale beyond knowing. What had once been disagreements and skirmishes among the people of this land there came times of slaughter with previously unknown cruelty. Spaniards brought diseases the people had not had before and more died than were left alive. As you know, a Spanish ship was blown to shore to the north. From this wreck, Spaniards are coming toward our village. The enemies' advance is being watched. People are starting to leave the village. You have made plans for me to leave with my sisters and their families. You and other men will wait here for the arrival of these enemies."

"After the battle," explained Stone Bear, "I want you to come with me when I go north to get more stone for making arrow points. I make them, as you know, from bone and shell but prefer stone. It is light, chips smoothly and makes sharp arrow points along with spear points and knives—even hoes or hatchets."

Holding the amulet attached by a leather cord around her neck, she said, "I cherish this stone bear you made for me. You drilled a hole through it so I can wear it. You got your name from the bears you carve."

"Everyone has a totem, or spirit, of an animal or bird as a guide," he explained. "My spirit guide is a bear and you have a connection to the great, white bird with the long feathers. I also enjoy the smaller, white bird because, like you, she keeps me company on the shore or canoe."

He stopped talking and started listening. Cries of gulls came from the sky above minnows that must have been spotted. A breeze stirred waves while rustling leaves of palms near the village where a murmur of people's voices could be heard as preparations were being made for the approaching enemies.

Most noticeable was the sound of waves first cresting then sending water plunging onto sand before returning back to be replaced by the next oncoming crest. This constant sound, by its permanence, gave comfort to all those who took time to listen.

Resting in the song of the sea, Stone Bear said to his wife, "Maybe you should get ready to leave with the others. I will join the men to defend our village.

According to reports, the enemy will be ready to attack next morning."

"I will be away for the night," replied White Bird. "Morning will come with its battle then we should travel north to get more stone."

The next morning, Stone Bear was aware there are times when the spirit becomes less noticeable, birds don't sing, the first light of day is only gray and the sun's rays bring no warmth. The Spaniards filled the open area circled by structures. Armed men arrived with weapons ready and were shocked by being met by only silence. It stalked the stillness and was as menacing as any enemy, particularly as it came by surprise.

Unnerved, the leader looked around then gazed to the tops of trees before shouting, "Come out. Come out and fight."

Also silent, was the reply. The leader staggered then fell back with an arrow protruding from his forehead just below the helmet. Soldiers scrambled amid a flurry of arrows. Screams filled the air, sounding particularly loud as they pierced previous silence.

Round after round of feathered shafts came from surrounding foliage and tops of palms. Some musket shots brought down a bowman. More arrows came seemingly in anger just before a wall of tattooed defenders charged from foliage flashing spear, club and knife, bringing death to those who brought it.

In a flurry of digging, a Spanish leader buried valuables that would slow a retreat soon to be called. A signal was given and soldiers tried to escape although the battle followed them. The enemies not directly slain by the Timucuans, were killed by the surrounding landscape.

After danger cleared away, as the passing of other storms, families returned to the village on the stretch of land facing the Gulf and backed by the entrance of a wide, freshwater stream. While others resumed old routines, Stone Bear and White Bird started walking northward.

Coolness of early morning gradually vanished. First light located minnows close to shore. Above them a cloud of birds gathered. Their cries filled the morning as rays of sunlight brought increased warmth.

"You missed your time to greet the new day while sipping hot drink from my pottery cup," observed White Bird.

"First light is not the only occasion to talk with the spirit world," he answered.

"That's the strength people see in you," noted White Bird.

"We are all spirits whether we know or not," he replied. "We work in the fields to grow our crops such as corn, beans, squash, potatoes and tobacco. You are celebrated for your pottery work. I make arrows and other weapons or tools. We all grow, gather and prepare food. Always there are stories. Some people only see these outward activities. I like to look further. Regardless of how far I look, the journey only begins. That's why I enjoy the spirit quest so much. I never get to the end. There's only the starting out. There are glimpses of such magnificence I keep searching for the next landmark. Everything has a purpose. We don't carry out our lives for nothing—as the enemies who attack us. They are not part of spirit life. They get only ashes and miss the fire."

"That's why I'm so attracted to you," said White Bird. "You are part of the spirit world. You say most of us are, although we don't see it. I'm always trying to understand you and never really getting there. This makes life so interesting."

"The excitement comes not just with the work we do each day but in searching and getting glimpses of why we do it," he exclaimed.

"The why we do it part is the most interesting aspect and you seek it each morning, while sipping hot drink from one of my cups," she observed.

"We understand each other," said Stone Bear, smiling.

"Walking with the company of a breeze stirring across the water curling waves onto the shore and rustling palm leaves is my favorite part of a day," she explained. "Maybe there is time now to enjoy the sea."

She removed her clothes, ran to the water and dove into a cresting wave, vanishing from view. Stone Bear also left his clothes on the sand and followed her. Swimming under the water, he saw her moving through golden wedges of sunlight. Swimming as gracefully as any fish, she surfaced to get air and Stone Bear came up beside her.

"We are in the world of water," she exclaimed. "It's as wild here as anywhere on land."

"Our homes are on land," he said. "We have to leave this wilderness to breathe as the other creatures also of or from the land."

"We must only take food respectfully," she continued, "and never take anything we don't actually need. But a turtle came up to breathe at the surface near us and we need food."

White Bird pointed to the place where the turtle had surfaced. Stone Bear swam down, gripped the creature's shell at the back near the neck. Kneeling, Stone Bear pulled upward. The turtle could now only swim to the surface before being steered to shore. A fire was started and the shell became a cooking pot for meat that was used immediately for food while more was dried on a rack for future use.

"The sun dips toward the west," noted White Bird. "Maybe we don't need a shelter. We could sleep beside the fire."

"Good idea," he agreed. "We have lots of food. We can rest, listen to waves, watch the sky and experience a fine night."

"We enjoy these wondrous days," mused White Bird. "Storms gather around us. The Calusa have also lost many people taken away by new diseases brought to our shores by the Spaniards. The newcomers' diseases kill more people than their swords. These enemies have trained dogs to hunt and kill us."

"We must gather the pleasures of one day at a time," he replied, "and each night."

Sleep came and brought a new day to the travelers. Their food supply lasted until they reached the warm spring surrounded by rocks. Other springs provided fresh water and supplied a large Timucuan village.

Stone Bear and White Bird drank the warm, smelling water for its health benefits but mainly used the occasion to float in the pool. They could drift, as if being on one of the clouds overhead moving across the sky far above all worries or fears.

"After resting, we could start following the trail to the place of the stone," suggested Stone Bear.

"I enjoy the work we do there," noted White Bird after his words came to her as if in a dream because she seemed to be soaring as an eagle, she watched moving on air currents far overhead. "I'm ready to start our journey again any time."

Leaving the place of springs the travelers moved inland, stopping only where they could get fresh water. In one place, approaching clouds warned that a good lean-to shelter would be needed. One was built with an enlarged cover extending partly over the fire. Stone Bear had shot a turkey and this large bird roasted on a spit above the flame as all around the shelter rain fell like a great falls of a river, spreading a white wall around camp and pounding the ground. Inside the circle of light from shelter's fire, there was warmth and food.

While tasting a slab of steaming, roasted meat, White Bird said, "Maybe there's no such thing as a bad day. This day could've been filled with trouble making us miserable but with a good shelter and delicious food I feel this whole time is a celebration of life."

After waiting at the camp for a few days, giving the trail a chance to dry, the journey continued. At a distant location, they prepared a camp close to the site where stone was to be gathered. Stone Bear removed the first chunks by a stone hammer and wooden prying pole. At camp, Stone Bear and White Bird broke large pieces into smaller sections to be gradually chipped into shapes designed to become arrow and spear points or tools.

When a sufficient supply was packed, Stone Bear and White Bird rested in preparation for the journey home. During the last night before leaving, the travelers sat beside their fire and White Bird said, "Unlike many people in our village, we have always enjoyed journeys to see new areas. Inland air is laced with fragrances of flowers added to scents of foliage and earth. Near the shores, vastness of water sends to land refreshing air currents touched by traces of salt or fish. The environment is everywhere beautiful. We have to prepare for storms yet broadening our scope of knowledge helps us to work through, over or around most obstacles. We are attracted to each place we visit. After seeing them with each wondrous aspect, there is always the knowledge providing a call reminding us only one place is home. We always want to return to our home on the long point of land with the inlet of water, starting as fresh stream before joining the sea. Our village site on this stretch of land with inlet on one side and sea on the other is a location where the Timucuans have lived for years beyond memory. The stream waters our crops and flows through fishponds under numerous bridges joining both banks while a special spring also supplies our village with good drinking water."

Looking at the comfortable camp heated by the fire, White Bird glanced to the realm beyond where a white spray of tumbling water nourished verdant slopes cloaked in mist. Her face clouded before she said, "I worry about the future after the arrival of warring Spaniards and the diseases these strangers bring. Many people have been leaving our village to stay away from this new threat approaching from the sea. Creeks have also been traveling southward. They join us who have lived here for countless years. Together we are sometimes called Seminoles."

"Time brings changes and we like to see different places," observed Stone Bear. "Among all worries or fears, only one place, our village by the stream and sea, has always had the unchanging call of home."

Chapter 3

The Settlers
1850

In front of the chickee huts, inside the Seminole village on the arm of land with the inlet on one side and ocean on the other, the leader, Ray Stonebear spoke to the villagers. When he spoke, others enjoyed listening. There was something about him that represented the land itself. He was of similar height and stature as other men. Yet his voice carried a message seeming to not just come from one person but a gathering together of all the land, water and people of the past. His dark eyes flashed in light from a central fire when he said, "None of us are old compared to our home on this special section of land bordered by an outlet of a freshwater stream on one side and sea on the other. People have seemingly—maybe—always lived here. We are often known as Seminoles. Mainly we are people from Creek villages to the north who have traveled southward. We have joined together with remnants of nations who have always called this region home. Dwellings of the Timucuans previously occupied our present village site. They joined us. I have received my name from Timucuan ancestors, White Bird and Stone

Bear. Others among us have ancestors who have always looked to Florida as their home. Among the devastation Spaniards brought to the first people living on this land, there are two things the strangers from across the sea did well. They called this area La Florida, Land of Flowers. The newcomers also brought oranges.

Amazing to realize that people who come lately to this land think those who have always lived here don't belong. The Americans have led two wars against us, trying to force us to move to western regions. We refused. Now a third attempt is being made.

People beyond anyone's memory have always called this site, between inlet and sea, home. In recent years some American settlers have moved close to us. I have talked to them. The man is called

Feston Sands and his wife is Jessica. They have no hostility toward us. Our home is here. We have two neighbors."

The central fire burned near the chickees in the Seminole village. People talked, gathering stories from the past and with them explained the present. The talk continued until the darkest part of night then the people in the village listened to a breeze rustling palms. This sound helped to bring sleep at the close of another wondrous day.

Rays of light from the early morning sun shone on the first people stirring in the village. Golden rays also brightened walls of a nearby cabin where Feston Sands prepared the day's first meal for himself and his wife, Jessica. He was always the first to greet a new day and this habit brought him naturally to the preparation of a meal.

Feston appeared to be as rugged as his cabin. His brown hair would be indistinguishable from his beard except for the fact his beard was mainly red. Out of this foliage, his nose protruded beyond his well-tanned face with unruly eyebrows and dark brown eyes.

"Thanks for the coffee," Jessica said to her husband, after she sat at the table where the first food and coffee of the day seemed always to be the best. After preparing the meal, Fes also sat on another chair next to the table. Sparse furnishings included two additional chairs, a bed, an extra table and cupboards.

Compared to her husband, Jessica appeared to be almost frail. She was slim. All her clothes seemed to fit loosely. Her hair was light brown and eyes dark blue. Casual observation could miss her inner strength that shone in her eyes and flashed in rare occasions of anger her husband dreaded because even her generally good humor could spear him with barbs from what even her friends called a sharp tongue.

"You really know how to treat a lady," observed Jessica.

"Oh, oh," he sighed. "I don't like the sound o' this—and so early in the morning, too."

"How could anyone ask for more?" she continued. "I appreciate being served coffee in the morning and sometimes corn cakes or flapjacks too. Those are luxuries I really do appreciate but there's a well too under our cabin where we get fresh water and I don't even think about the insects that fall in there along with maybe a small animal, lizard or snake. Who could complain about a bit o' snake poop in the coffee? Who needs more than this cabin? We have glass windows on the east and west sides to let in light. Palm logs are chinked with Spanish moss. We have cups we received in trade with our Seminole neighbors. I would like to know them better but they stay away from us because the government has been trying to force them out of Florida and has started a third Seminole war. I like the coontie flour we get from them in exchange for coffee. We get extra amounts for them. We shoot alligators and use hides like money to purchase supplies. We haul muck from swampy places to fertilize our crops of corn, beans, squash and potatoes."

Jessica stopped talking to sip coffee then looked around at their cabin with the day's first sunlight entering through the glass window and spreading a path of golden color along a wall. "I started off by complaining," she mused, "but as I consider everything we are both lucky to be here."

"I usually see through your barbs and jabs—complaints," replied Fes. "This might seem to be just a small, rough cabin but it shelters us from rain and cold—or bugs and some other critters like snakes or alligators. We actually live in the world's greatest mansion of the surrounding landscape. Its magnificence increases as our awareness grows. The longer we live here the more we see of surrounding beauty."

"I think I'll work in our garden today," noted Jessica.

"When the first light was seeping into the dawn, I heard a lot of popping sounds of shooting coming from the southeast at the Seminole village," explained Fes. "There's the smell of smoke in the air. I think I'll see what has happened."

"Better to know what's going on," she agreed.

After serving corn bread and more coffee, Feston left the cabin as Jessica prepared to work in the garden. He walked to the southeast, heading toward the village. A mockingbird sang almost constantly sending out a variety of melodies. Added to this background music, calls of cardinals rang from branches of long leaf pines. Feston walked under branches of majestic live oaks just before he came to the inlet where a wide expanse of fresh water flowed slowly toward the Gulf.

He started to cross where the stream was somewhat shallow although very wide. He had crossed at the same place numerous times and knew the bottom was firm along with being sandy. The water was also quite clear and mainly fresh since a salt mixture usually did not come this far upstream.

He was in the deepest section when a shot fired from the far side sent up a plumb of spray beside his face. To avoid other shots, he dove into the stream then looked around at the watery world of muted colors. Sunlight sparkled on the surface while sending wedges of golden hues through the water. All colors became lost in a generally dark blue haze of distance.

Out of the darker realm, there swam a man who held a knife in one hand. Feston went to the surface, gulped air then re-entered the water in time to see the man swimming down after also going up for air.

Coming directly at Feston, the knife flashed in sunlight in a passing swipe that Feston avoided then he grabbed the attacker's wrist before the two men grappled, struggling to subdue the other. They splashed through the surface, gulped air and one said, "Ray?"

"Fes?" asked the other.

"Why are you attacking me?" asked Feston.

"Didn't recognize you," Ray Stonebear replied. "Soldiers attacked our village at first light this morning. Most of our people had already left. We knew we could no longer stay at the village. We are moving to a more secure home. You looked like just another attacker."

"I thought I heard shots—and smelled smoke," replied Fes. "I was going to see what had happened."

"We knew we had to leave and I've been thinking you should claim our village site for your home," offered Ray.

"I don't want to benefit from your loss," countered Fes.

"Someone will occupy that location," stated Ray. "I have talked about this with the others. We would rather have a friendly neighbor there rather than a stranger we, and the land, would not welcome. We move to make our home more secure. You could also move your home to a better site. Make your claim. With you there, we can come back to visit so we do not leave."

"Very thoughtful and kind of you," stated Fes.

"We both win," said Ray. "And make the best of this situation."

"If people would only get to know their neighbors," whispered Fes.

"With you there we can visit our previous home and now we move to a more secure place," repeated Ray.

"Thank you for your explanation and confidence," said Fes. "You have helped me to change locations."

"The land knows you and we do too," stated Ray. "Although we did not meet you often."

"Ray!" came a clear voice from the far bank. "Are you going to fight him or talk him to death?"

"He's Feston Sands," replied Ray then silence followed except for resumed songs of mockingbirds and cardinals.

"That was my wife," explained Ray.

"We haven't met often but come back," said Fes.

"We will continue our journey," observed Ray. "Make your claim."

"And make your visit," added Fes, before both men turned and started walking back toward their homes.

When Fes reached his cabin, Jessica was not inside. He walked to their small crops and saw her working. "Would you like some sassafras tea?" he asked.

"Call when you are ready," she answered.

He walked to the cabin, prepared the drinks and carried them to a shaded area provided by a long leaf pine. When they were both resting, sipping tea from mugs, Fes said, "A lot has happened."

"Good news, I hope?" she asked.

"I wonder if all news is good depending only on the way we see it?" he replied.

"This doesn't sound good," she stated, as she looked at him directly with her eyes darker than usual—a color of worry.

"As I mentioned this morning," he explained, "I heard shots and smelled smoke coming from the area where the Seminole village is located. To see what had happened, I was crossing the inlet when someone shot at me from the opposite shore. To avoid more shots, I dove beneath the surface where I saw, swimming toward me a guy with a knife. We fought under water until we both had to surface to breathe and we recognized each other. The guy was Ray Stonebear. He thought I was one of the soldiers who attacked his village. The villagers have recently been moving to a more secure location. The last people were leaving when attacked.

"Ray said we have been good neighbors and the people of the village would like us to move our home to their abandoned site. This would place a friend on that land so the site would remain a home they could visit. They are traveling to a more secure area and we could move to a place where a breeze keeps away flies that are a problem for us at our cabin located farther inland. We would have closer access to the ocean for fishing. Are you willing to move? The ocean shore awaits."

"I'm sorry our neighbors are moving," she replied, "but you have described a way they can stay and we can remain also—and in a better location."

"That's a 'yes'?" he asked.

"Yes," she said. "I think you and Ray have drawn as much justice as can be saved from an unjust situation."

"The right and wrong in life is often not ours to arrange but we can only choose the most justice out of what is available," added Fes.

"The unfairness dampens my excitement about moving to a better location," observed Jessica.

"The change of location was offered to us," noted Fes.

"And our neighbors continue to be present as they have been since any records have been kept," confirmed Jessica.

"We agree," he concluded. "Our home will now be beside the sea and the freshwater stream. My first task is to start out on a journey and claim that section of land."

"We have a lot of work to do," she said. "Let's make the claim, build the new cabin then move stuff over."

"That's what the days and nights now will find us doing," he noted, looking out into the distance where there were plans that maybe were always there and he was just now seeing them.

"What do you see?" she enquired.

"Our life," he answered.

"Is it ours to invent or to follow?" she wondered aloud.

"The main outlines seemed to be already in place and, at times such as this, we see them if we are looking," observed Fes. "Our reactions to the journey remain ours to make and thereby we determine our path or life."

"I see the joy presented to us," she mused. "I also am aware of greatness lost. The Indigenous people have lived here for so long they are part of this land. The Spaniards brought havoc both by invasion and disease, reducing the first populations by maybe sixty to seventy percent. So much greatness in numbers of people and heritage has been lost. Imagine the wondrous possibilities that could've resulted if our governments had embraced differences rather than attacked them? We are all less because of such losses. Reactions of others affect us. We can only attempt to make our own best decisions then enjoy the wondrous results of right paths through life. We welcomed our neighbors rather than attacking them and as a result of our choices we have achieved—acquired—so much beauty. We are being invited to share land between sea and inlet and we have friends. Although life is a struggle we can make it better or worse."

"Your agreement with moving has covered a lot of information," exclaimed Fes. "I see the beauty and greatness in what you are outlining. The soldiers attacked the Seminoles and the loss of people and heritage is beyond perception. We have welcomed our neighbors. Our lives are so much happier and richer because of our actions."

"On days such as this we at least can feel assured we are on the right trail," mused Jessica. "Do we make the route or just follow it? The main course we don't make when we are on this earth. Likely we establish the outlines of what we want to achieve before we arrive. After we have come here we try to make the best decisions. Our work each day or night is to try our best. We must not turn away but walk the trail. You are I agree about the main journey. We have to have faith. I married the right person."

"I've always known I did too," he added, "our home just got bigger."

"We must make the claim then build a new cabin," she noted.

"If we had home brew this is the time we could be celebrating," he declared.

"I hope the Seminoles are celebrating too," she said.

"I think they are," offered Fes. "They are safer and that's a wonderful feeling to have—actually an essential aspect to making a place a home. The land is beautiful and not just in one place. The more we become aware, the more magnificence we see—and it can be almost everywhere even if it's in a memory or in the future. Nothing lasts forever except the spiritual world, the home of the Creator."

"You see a lot for a rough, tough, hairy, bearded, guy," she exclaimed.

"Somewhere in there, I think that might have been a compliment," he observed, smiling.

"They don't come often; so better to not miss them," she replied.

"Occasionally, I see what you already know," he declared.

"Another compliment," she said. "That's enough for a while. Let's get back to work. Maybe I could travel with you to make the claim."

They traveled to the settlement and upon returning started working on the new building. As always, Fes first set down a mortar and shell foundation in preparation for the next sections of palm logs. The new cabin was built much like the other. Any moveable furnishings were put into the new site. They took special care with the cooking facilities completed with the Dutch oven.

The Seminole village had been supplied with fresh water from a spring. This source provided the best coffee and tea. When all parts of old and new had been gathered, comforts only dreamed about at the previous site could now be enjoyed. Breezes from the sea mainly kept away mosquitoes and this aspect was welcomed more than most others. Previously, times of rest at the end of a day's work often had to be enjoyed inside the structure. Now both Jessica and Fes sat on chairs located in front of the new building and rested while enjoying the sea. Almost always, the vast expanse of water sent to shore a stir of air laced with a scent of salt along with fish. Porpoises moved past out beyond a sand bar. Pelicans patrolled above the waves.

Jessica and Fes became seafaring people. When they truly discovered the Gulf it became their way of life. They learned about the tides, collected shells and added fish to meals almost every day. The new seafarers also got to know the water world with all its changing moods, starting with sunrise when sky and water gathered an endless assortment of colors from the warming rays. While the sun traveled across the sky, hues faded until midday when there was the greatest heat and brightness. As afternoon advanced colors reappeared, painting uniquely each part of the day until evening approached and colors deepened to gradually become the darker shades of night.

Jessica and Fes not only got to know the sea but it became acquainted with them—and accepted them. The heron and egret became sentinels decorating either the cabin's roof or chairs in front facing the beach. Lizards moved to the new building and enjoyed its outer and inner walls. Cries of gulls became a natural sound of the sea while cardinals sang from live oaks and long leaf pines near the cabin.

Gator hunting continued to obtain hides used like currency for purchasing supplies. Fishing became a main method of getting food. All shoreline kinds of fish were abundant.

After the new cabin was finished and the move from the previous site had been completed, Jessica and Feston sat on chairs in front of their home and sipped home brew purchased at the settlement. "A new life begins for us," observed Jessica. "Looking back we can see that our journey here was part of our life all the time. We just could not see ahead as far as we can look back."

"We both feel welcome at this location," added Fes. "The water world has accepted us as we enjoy being here. All the time we have been people of the sea. We lived mainly in the inland wilderness. We have discovered that the sea is just as wild and less known, adding to a mystery that brings to each day a new discovery. The section of Timucuan gill net I found in the sand and we now have added to a wall of our cabin reminds us of new ways of acquiring food. With our next load of gator hides I'll buy nets both gill and cast. I have sufficient lines and hooks.

With our most recent bunch of hides I bought the boards and other equipment for making our boat with oars and a sail."

"Food here is abundant," noted Jessica. "There's the usual food on land with the razor backs or wild hogs along with turkeys and ibises. We have a new garden planted in muck beside the fresh water inlet where we grow corn and tomatoes. We can soon enjoy fried tomatoes or sandwiches made with bread using the settlement's flour or the Seminoles' coontie. Now that we are growing corn we can start making more corn cakes or bread."

"Mainly," said Fes, while he gazed out to sea, "I'm going to become a fisherman. I'll use line and hook along with nets."

Florida

Fes and Jessica moved naturally not only from one cabin to another but from one land based realm to a new world of the sea. The sea called Jessica and Fes and drew them to itself, revealing its secrets seen by a select group. Birds became constant companions, particularly the pairs of herons and egrets. Land animals appeared more often even including the elusive wolf.

Fes lived, in particular, with the Gulf. He learned to know the winds and currents. After work was completed, his finest moments came when he stepped into his small boat, set the sail to catch the breeze, and became part of the sea. With water splashing against the bow, wind in the sail, he let the sea take him away to become connected to something so much larger than himself. At such times he relaxed completely while he joined a song of wind and water. During these occasions he rested and dreamed.

One day, after returning from one of his visits with the sea, Fes said to Jessica. "There is difficulty in trying to take food to other people at the settlement because most things spoil before they reach such a destination. We could, however, bring people here. We should build the Sands Lodge."

"After you made the boat," replied Jessica, "I realized that people could visit us by boat. To accommodate visitors, we would have to expand our cabin and right now this possibility is beyond our resources."

"Someday," mused Fes, "a lodge will be one of those projects saved for someday."

"The meal is ready," said Jessica. "Today we have oyster stew with new corn bread I just made."

"People would come to our lodge just for your cooking," exclaimed Fes, before they walked toward their cabin.

While enjoying the meal, Fes said, "Our main food has become fish. Turkeys are numerous around the inlet. We have been enjoying the oysters. This stew is delicious. Oysters are also good fried. Frog legs are certainly now available. Mainly we have fish and most kinds of them particularly the mackerel. The Seminoles were repairing the very old Timucuan fish weir at the inlet. I could finish working on that also, if we ever needed more food. The Timucuans appear to have had fishponds joining the stream. Now we can catch, easily, whatever we want."

"When we lived inland at our previous cabin," observed Jessica, "we did not realize we were just naturally people of the sea. The water calls to us at this site. We have heard and answered. Maybe some people are just natural seafarers. I could watch the water all day long and night too. The Gulf never rests even when it appears to be calm. There are always currents and so much life under the surface. The vast open spaces send to shore varying breezes not to mention the stronger winds. I like all types of waves and can sleep best at night within the sound of water crashing along the shore. Birds are endlessly interesting although we enjoyed the inland varieties also. We continue to get the cardinals here but I miss the varying calls of mockingbirds."

"The fire at this Seminole village not only burned chickees but also a bordering area of brush," noted Fes. "Such a clearing of land has uncovered new features of terrain long hidden by foliage. Plants are emerging."

"Our neighbors will have found a new home they enjoy just as we have," mused Jessica. "I continue to regret, however, the way the Seminoles were forced from homes known to Indigenous nations longer than any records can tell the story. We are all poorer for this loss. We have come to an understanding with the people yet the ashes on the ground are one loss while the ashes of lost heritage is another matter and a much greater—even incalculable loss to us all. We have to stop the absurdity of fearing differences. There are no two things on earth that are the same—no two people, or two birds or trees or blades of grass. The only common link is the Creator. The Native Americans were communicating with the Creator for thousands of years before the arrival of the Europeans."

"Ashes of lost heritage and richness of life," mused Fes, "are something I'll think about the next time I check the burned over ground. I like to watch the new growth emerging. I wish the lost achievements and potentials of people could return as quickly."

"With our life here," replied Jessica, "I keep remembering the loss. I wonder if the cultures of the Timucuans and other Florida nations will always be lost or in the wider scope of life does heritage also grow back like the new plants emerging from ashes on the ground?"

While watching young plants emerging, even thriving, in burned areas, Fes noticed that a circular patch of earth had dropped down below bordering ridges, revealing a possibility that a small pit had been dug here and the earth through years had resettled to a new natural level.

Curious, he started digging inside the lower circle. Some roots had to be chopped and removed by using an ax. Most of the soil was sand comprised of small or broken shells.

"You should be careful," warned Jessica. "There are underground rivers in Florida. Maybe a flow of water caused a small sink hole. I should put a rope on you."

"If I start going down, I'll climb out and get a rope," he joked.

"That's planning ahead," she countered. "What would you like on your grave marker?"

"He's home," he replied.

Fes resumed digging and stopped when one end of a rope dropped on him. "The other end is tied to a palm," she explained.

After securing the rope, he started working again until the shovel clanked against a barrier, sounding metallic.

"I'm tied up here," he shouted to Jessica. "Please bring me a prying pole."

Using this additional tool, he loosened an object then forced it to the surface. After climbing out of the hole, he probed the object with the shovel's blade until he stopped and shouted, "This thing is a rusted helmet—a Spanish helmet. Must've been buried by soldiers who had extra stuff they did not want to—or could not—carry any farther."

"You have uncovered the past," she exclaimed. "What a story you have found and maybe it has just started. Keep turning the pages of your digging into the past."

He went back to work until uncovering a larger form of rusted metal and exclaimed, "Has to be a breastplate—Spanish armor. They likely had too much stuff to carry and were in a hurry. They were forced to leave quickly and this stuff would just slow them down. The Indigenous nations of the Americas would have thriving cities today if the Spaniards had been forced to leave the first day they arrived. In earlier times, there was a Timucuan village here. The Spaniards would have attacked them and were forced to retreat quickly. They buried what they couldn't carry in a rush and didn't want this stuff to be found by those they fought."

"I hope this story isn't over," said Jessica. "Maybe there's more to be told."

Fes returned to his work. When sounds of digging stopped, Jessica, feeling some worry, walked to the pit, looked inside and saw Fes sitting, surrounded by an array of objects—some large and many small.

"I'm not sure I believe it," he said, looking up at her. "These objects are the heaviest and could not be carried by people who had to travel rapidly. The large chunks are gold bars. The smaller things are gold coins. Beauty surrounds us everywhere in this wondrous environment. These pieces are not attractive yet they sure have value—and are worth a lot more than alligator hides. We have gold."

Jessica jumped into the hole and picked up one of the smaller objects. "Only gold would be that heavy," she whispered.

"I've scraped them with the shovel and did some probing with my knife," he added. "We have gold coins and bars. We must plan wisely so this discovery is good news and not trouble."

"What a wonderful problem to have," she whispered. "I agree with you. We have to plan carefully to ensure we direct a fortune in a way to have it become good news and not a disaster. Maybe we should cover everything over and do some talking."

"Good idea," he replied before they both stepped out of the hole. "Want to come for a swim? I want to wash off some sweat and grime."

With thoughts on a discovery that seldom comes if at all to anyone, Feston and Jessica walked out into the more awesome world of warming sunlight where a gentle breeze brought small waves splashing along the shore with a constantly repeated song that made life by the water more restful than any other realm. Sunrays seemed to reduce all sharp colors and fade the environment with brightness of light.

After leaving clothes on the sand, Fes and Jessica dove into the waves. Beneath the surface, the initial, shallow areas were painted golden by sunlight. Deeper regions added greenish hues that became lost in gradually increasing blueness of distance. Through these colors, particularly the more distant blues, a school of mackerel swam past. Without seeming to move in any other way other than straight ahead, the sleek fish all darted onward like one living creature.

Most of the time, mused Fes, *people don't really see the world of water because we only watch its surface. Beneath the waves there's as much diversity of life as there is above. When in the water, I prefer to be under it.*

Jessica swam past, moving gracefully and appearing to belong to the world of water until she left it to breathe. Fes also submerged then splashed back to the realm of sky and sunlight.

As Jessica gazed around at life above the surface, she said, "We are elated because we have found gold. The real gold, in other words riches is in this magnificent wilderness."

"We are so lucky to see such a place and actually live here," agreed Feston. "Gold bars and coins only help to obtain supplies and build structures. The wilderness is formed not just in physical aspects but also with a continuing spiritual presence infused by the builder, the Creator. No coins are available to establish a wilderness. No one can build a spirit."

"Too much of a nation's interests center on things people are doing," observed Feston. "Often overlooked is our understanding of what has already been done and is arrayed all around us and this is the natural world. The main part of our efforts should be in protecting our environment and not in congratulating ourselves for cutting it down, digging it up or otherwise polluting the natural world in what we consider to be progress. Why do we admire loggers who cut down a forest? Such an action should be considered a crime. Use but don't destroy should be our policy rather than waste then move on as if the supply of wilderness is endless. It is limited. We wreck it at our own peril."

"Our disagreements are small and our agreements are vast as they are endless and that is how we got married," noted Jessica. "I would like to hear your opinion of what we should do with the gold coins and bars."

"Do you mind if I catch you a fish and serve you a meal before offering you some suggestions?" asked Fes.

"You can catch and prepare meals any time," she answered.

They returned to the shore of sand where they put clothes back on and Fes said, "As a different choice, could I prepare you a meal after we go for a walk while I mention some ideas I have as to what to do with the coins and bars?"

"I'd like to hear your thoughts and as soon as possible," she replied. "I can't stop thinking about what we found."

They started to walk along the shore, stepping on sand where it had the firmness of being constantly dampened by waves sending water rushing landward then flowing back to the base of the next onrush. Sandpipers searched for food in moving sheets of water. Gulls and terns dove for minnows while pelicans patrolled just above the waves.

Feston and Jessica knew they did not live or walk alone. Today a breeze lazed by traces of salt and fish brought freshness and moved palms back from the stretch of shoreline. Clouds drifted across a seemingly endless blue sky where a frigate bird soared. Always there was the favorite companion of the sea. Tying together and filling all parts there continued the spiritual presence shining through life.

"We have found," said Fes, "a large supply of money. The question is—who owns it? Spaniards must have lost a battle and had to retreat in a hurry. So they buried what was a burden to carry, planning to return later.

It is not Spanish gold although many people call it that. Such wealth was stolen from Native Americans farther south where cities were ransacked and pillaged. I have heard those cities had libraries and hospitals.

We found Indian gold. The Seminoles, who included other Indian nations previously living in Florida, lived here until the part of their home that is farther inland offered more security. This is Indian land.

We are one of three owners. I suggest to you we divide the gold into three equal parts. Two parts will be given to Ray Stonebear and his wife on behalf of the Seminoles and the Indian owners. We could keep one third. We should use this to hire a crew who can build a row of cabins that will be a lodge. We will live in one cabin and rent the others to people who could arrive by boat. We will run a lodge. Someday our sons and daughters can take over. We could call the place, the Sands Lodge.

Ray Stonebear and his wife, Orchid, plan to come here to visit us and enjoy again this part of their home. At that time we will give them two bags or two thirds of the gold. This will help them build structures as it helps us. That's my suggestion."

After speaking, Fes gazed again out at the sea then watched waves breaking along the sand while birds moved in the sky. Following a long silence, Jessica said, "I knew—and hoped—you would see it that way. I'm pleased there is a part we can keep for our lodge. There is so much we don't own such as almost everything except our own spirits. That's all we take with us when we go home to our spiritual world from whence we came. We don't own the gold, or land—sky—water—birds. We are visitors—bystanders—and we must only be here to improve our spirits because we don't even own our own bodies that get left behind when we leave to go home. We leave the way we arrived—as spirits—and that's all we have when we go back. What a vain enterprise it is to try building great accumulations of wealth upon this earth although some adds comfort to life rather than unnecessary hardship.

"We have no wealth if it is the property of others. We have only what belongs to us. That's the part where we have choices as to what we could or should do. I agree with you. Only one third is ours. This we can use as seems best. A lodge is our best choice. First we'll have the dinner you mentioned. Afterward we'll hire a crew. They and supplies will come in by boat."

"Life has shifted," said Fes. "Everything is now so different for us you could almost expect that the environment might also change. It hasn't. The world of sky, water and land goes on like previously. Pelicans fly past looking for fish. Gulls too follow the same quest. Sandpipers run across the sand, searching flows of water for food. Gives you an idea of the magnitude of life when you realize an enormous change for us has apparently not altered life around us."

"I like your ideas about ownership," stated Jessica. "They feel right."

"We agree and I have some fishing to do," he concluded.

After walking, Fes carried his fishing equipment to the water's edge where he met his two usual companions the snowy egret and great blue heron. Fes threw out the net to catch minnows. First he fed his partners then baited a line. The first catch was a slender ladyfish that went to the heron. A second ladyfish filled this fisherman. With a croak to signal departure, outstretched wings carried this fisherman back to the roof of the cabin. The egret, also full of minnows, left shortly afterward and returned to the other half of the roof. Following a longer wait, Fes also had sufficient food with the catch of a large mackerel. He carried it to the back of the cabin for filleting.

Jessica and Feston dined on fillets fried to a golden color followed by tea while the sun dipped into haze at the horizon, becoming an orange orb. Colors of sunset deepened with the approach of night.

Resting in the beauty of their surroundings with a warm breeze blowing in from the ocean along with a background song of waves breaking along the shore, Fes and Jessica slept on the sand, awakening to see first rays of sunlight announce a special day. Following a meal of corn cakes and coffee, the two people, with dreams of a new lodge, traveled to the nearest community to hire a crew.

Travel by boat brought workers and supplies to first put down a base comprised of mortar and shells. Flooring came next followed by walls and roofs.

The lodge was becoming a presence by the shore when Fes and Jessica went for one of their walks. No walk was the same as the others. One day in particular they were returning and followed by two people in a dugout canoe.

Near the lodge, the paddlers brought their craft to shore. The man got out and pulled the craft part way up on the sand before the woman stepped out to stand beside him. She was slim and moved with grace. Her black hair was long and face narrow, showing beauty and strength. There seemed to be a reserve or hostility flashing in her eyes.

"We have waited for your arrival," said Feston, in greeting Ray and Orchid Stonebear. "Returning from our walk, we have immediately started preparing a meal."

"Thank you," replied Ray before they all walked to a shelter near the cabin where Jes and Fes lived. Their cabin was at the outer edge of a row of similar structures. Jes and Fes offered a meal of corn cakes along with roasted fish followed by tea.

"Thank you for your hospitality," said Orchid. "I have met you briefly but Ray has told me much about you. We brought you coontie flour that we know you enjoy. You have planted something interesting here."

"And you are part of the something interesting," observed Fes. "We have waited for a long time to tell you a story."

"Ray is one of our best story tellers," stated Orchid, smiling for the first time. "He is a keeper of our records, a holder of our legends about this land and our people."

"The fire in your village that was located here burned some adjacent brush and foliage," explained Fes. "In the ground left bare there was a dip where the surface sand had dropped down away from surrounding sides. Curious as to what had caused this disturbance, I dug down. The shovel hit something hard. It was a Spanish helmet. Spaniards must have lost a battle here many years ago when this was a Timucuan village site. The soldiers apparently had to retreat quickly. Not being able to carry burdensome supplies while moving swiftly, more awkward items were buried with the intention of returning for them later.

I started digging again. The shovel scrapped against a larger object. It turned out to be a breastplate. Beneath that there were gold coins and bars."

"Wow," exclaimed Ray, smiling. "That explains the construction around here."

"Yes," said Jessica. "We are building cabins—a lodge—for visitors to come here and enjoy the area."

Turning to look more closely at Fes, she asked, "Do you want to continue?"

"This is your turn," he replied.

To her guests, she continued saying, "This area is part of your home—you and the Seminoles who include some of the earlier nations living in Florida such as the Timucuans. The gold was stolen from the Native Americans and also this is your land. So we divided the coins and bars into three equal bags. We are keeping one lot as the finders of it and using it to build this lodge. The gold is Native American as is this land. Thereby you are getting two of the three equal bags. We thought this was fair and hope you do also."

Ray and Orchid looked at each other. Silently they spoke, saying more at once than words would ever express. The only visible result of the exchange was the disappearance of hard hostility from Orchid's eyes.

"We did not expect this," said Orchid. "Such deep justice usually does not come from people who have journeyed more recently to this land."

"Spaniards buried this gold," continued Fes, "however, they did not own it. They stole it when they burned Indian cities to the south. This is Indian gold because they found it first."

Ray and Orchid looked at each other again, speaking silently, before Orchid said, "This is much more than would be expected. Why does so much justice come now?"

"Not everyone brings justice," replied Ray. "The physical might fail but the spirit never does. The Creator is always present yet in times of trouble we don't always see the presence."

"You seem to see more often than others," observed Orchid.

"During those times when I saw, I married you," he added.

Orchid's face brightened and light flashed between her and her husband.

Turning to look at Fes and Jes, Orchid said, "You must see the light too because you have shared this discovery with the other two owners."

Seeing the glow brightening Ray's face and the glint in his eyes, Orchid knew he was up to something. He lowered his head and looked at the ground as if in its company he gathered his thoughts. Looking up at his two friends, he said, "You could be the first newcomers off the boats who actually paid for the land they received. First you were friends and good neighbors. Now you help us buy back some of our losses. We will talk to the others. This area of land where your lodge is located will be your property. Land of the Sand's lodge will belong to the Sands family. You have paid for it. This will be remembered. We keep records and legends tell our story."

Florida

"Fes mentioned this plan to me," said Jessica, "and when I heard it, I felt a peacefulness return to me that had vanished when we found the gold. I at first felt there was something sinister in what we had uncovered. Now that feeling has gone—been driven out be something so much stronger."

"Wow," exclaimed Orchid. "Gold is a 'wow', but the greater 'wow' is what we have met here, not physical richness but something more wondrous. The wealth of what you've done with the gold is so much greater than the stuff you dug up."

"Wow," said Jessica. "You should have visited us more often when you were at the village."

"We met you often enough to know who you were," replied Orchid.

"I got an idea Ray's wife was not someone to be overlooked," added Fes, "when she shouted across the water to Ray, saying, 'Are you going to fight him or talk him to death?'"

"It was Orchid who shot at you," said Ray. "You're lucky. We are all lucky because I would not have missed."

"Imagine what the government would achieve if they didn't shoot," observed Jessica.

"Shooting is necessary in self-defense," said Ray.

"Yes—but not if self-defense means being the aggressor," noted Orchid. "Only victims can shoot in self-defense—not the oppressors or destroyers."

"Maybe I should show you the two bags," suggested Feston. He walked away and returned carrying a shovel. He removed sand revealing two leather bundles. They were hauled out and opened.

"Much good will come of this," noted Orchid.

"We should get it back to the others," suggested Ray.

"Can we help?" asked Fes.

"You have already helped," answered Orchid. "Now, Ray and I must bring assistance to others."

The four people took the bundles to the dugout. After Ray and Orchid stepped inside their craft, Jessica said, "We appreciate the coontie."

"We appreciate what we've seen here today," replied Orchid, "and I'm not just talking about what is in these two bags. There have been times when I think what we've seen here today no longer exists until flashes occur and I can carry on."

"While we were traveling here," said Ray, "we could not know we would journey so much further than the distance covered by walking and paddling to this particular part of shore where a lodge is being planted and will be growing." Paddles dipped into the water and the craft started to return the way it had come.

Watching the two people leaving, Jessica said to her husband, "If all days were like this, would life be too easy?"

"No," he replied. "We have to climb the mountain to see the view."

"The view is always there, though," she said, "and we should try to remember that all those times when we can't see it."

"I'll never forget the view we saw today," observed Fes, "and we all saw it."

After the craft with the two paddlers had moved out of sight, Fes said, "Ray mentioned that we were planting a lodge. Maybe we should help it grow and get back to work."

"Tomorrow," responded Jessica. "Today, I've been somewhere I don't want to leave."

"We won't leave," he noted. "Ray and Orchid won't forget either. They have something to plant—like us."

Resting on sand in front of their cabin, Fes and Jessica watched the sun move to the completion of a day that had been unforeseen yet would never be forgotten. "There are days such as this," said Jessica, "when we walk in the spirit more than on the ground. When we do this all the time, we will no longer be on the ground. Maybe the lodge will be one of the markers we leave behind, to mark the trail of our lives."

While the lodge, having been planted, was helped to grow by the work crew, Fes visited the cook at their tent camp and returned, as often occurred with some food roasted for that day's main meal. Bringing back a special meal of roasted hog, along with a bottle of home brew, he greeted Jessica in front of their cabin. Jessica added some tea and coontie bread before they sat to enjoy a celebration of one of the best of times.

"Our favorite food is fried fish," offered Fes. "Hog is a treat when one of the workers shoots one. The coontie bread is special."

"Life is a constant struggle against one difficulty after another," explained Jessica. "Hardship we know so well we stop considering life any other way except during a few special days when the sun, beginning its downward slope to mark afternoon, adds golden light to blue sky where clouds drift along with high-flying, well fed pelicans and the usual frigate bird—and all parts seem to suddenly, in a flash of light or insight, fall into place and we see the presence of the Creator. This presence we can't see during trouble when light is needed most. Yet during this special time, I see all parts are as they should be and we are exactly where we are meant to be. I'm happy today."

"Try some of the workers' home brew," offered Fes, giving her a full glass.

"Thank you," she replied. "This will help us sleep—maybe here on the sand where we can more clearly listen to the most restful sound I've ever heard and that's the steady splash of waves tumbling onto the shore."

The sun dropped into a slight haze above the horizon. As the orb dipped lower, it gathered to itself red hues before gradually vanishing and drawing away most light that was not replaced until the moon sent a silver trail to the sandy shore where two people slept. Farther up on high ground, silver light also etched a lodge. It too had life and like a living plant had grown almost to its full size. At the back of this row of cabins there was a sign proclaiming the new structure to be "Sands Lodge".

Morning sunlight found the two lodge owners enjoying a breakfast of flapjacks at a table in front of their cabin. A cooking fire was also burning near tents used by the work crew.

Feston and Jessica had just completed their meal and poured coffee when the crew foreman, Jack Dooley, walked toward the table.

"Just in time," said Fes to the approaching man. "Sit and enjoy some coffee."

"Thank you," he replied, accepting a cup before sitting. His hair and beard provided a scruffy outline to a face weathered through many storms and covered by sunlight with a dark tan. He moved with the ease of a person who was at home anywhere but inside a building.

"This is the kind o' work the men and I like," he stated. "Build the cabins all in a row—making sort o' one building. Supplies can come by boat almost up to where they are needed. The surroundings are beautiful. While we are here, we feel as if we are on holidays. We even catch fish for meals. Shot some turkeys also along with hogs and one cougar. Hide will go on my wall at home—to accompany the two wolf pelts. Such furs are hard to come by any more. Shot the cougar when it was raiding our pig snare. Got one wolf, left it until the second appeared then shot it. Such hides are getting scarcer all the time. Maybe the days of living off wild game are coming to an end."

"We'll always have fish if we don't take too many," offered Jessica, "along with farm or ranch-raised food such as cows, chickens and pigs."

"I've been shooting wild pigs," noted Jack. "They root around back of the outhouses. Maybe they are attracted to the inlet for its fresh water."

After taking a gulp of coffee, he asked, "You always pay for everything using old, gold coins?"

"Yes," answered Fes, "as long as they last. They should take us to the time when the lodge opens."

"We've been talkin' to people about this place," noted the foreman, "and looks as if you're goin' to get lots o' customers—mainly fishermen. Many of the crew want to return for some more fishing. Boar hunting around here is good too. Each time we get one, we roast the whole critter on a spit over the fire—and we'll always make sure you get some. You should join us for a dinner."

"We'd enjoy that," replied Jessica. "We'll bring my specialty of corn cakes or biscuits."

"Just like home," said Jack, smiling. "As I said, this place is my preferred type of job. I am, though, at home anywhere I'm outside. We're making good progress. This happens when the men live—enjoy being—where they work."

"Do you have all the supplies you need?" asked Feston.

"The last boat is on its way now," answered the foreman. "We'll soon have everything you've requested. Your residence is of course here at this cabin. The other structures for visitors are being completed. They each have an inside and outside fireplace along with interior wood stove in addition to a Dutch oven. Water is piped in from the spring to a sink and cooking area. There's the one central room with two adjoining bedrooms. An outhouse is at the back of each cabin and there's a rowboat in front. Of course there are chairs, tables and cupboards. Visitors can look after themselves in each cabin. People will come here to fish and enjoy the beach."

"You've included everything," noted Jes, before she gave Jack a leather pouch. "This is an extra bonus for you and your other workers."

"Your generosity is appreciated," exclaimed Jack, standing. "You are doing your best. I'd better do the same and get back to work. The men will be happy with this bonus."

The foreman walked back to talk to the crew. Happy shouts followed his visit to each one as he distributed the extra payment.

"A good foundation is set not just by mortar and shells but, more importantly, by happy people," observed Fes.

"I have a good feeling about this place," added Jessica. "This is the first time I've had an awareness of not wanting to go anywhere else. The farther I walk away the more I want to return as if this is the place I've been traveling to all my life. I'm here now and all parts fit into harmony that is partially broken when I move away even a short distance. I am aware of not being home when I move out from here. At least this site is right for me—where everything is in place."

"I have the same attitude," agreed Fes. "We've thrown our anchor out here. Others can come and stay at the cabins."

"We are calling our home 'Sands Lodge'?" inquired Jessica.

"Do you agree with 'Sands Lodge'?" he checked.

"Has a good sound to it," she replied. "Maybe one of the crew is a carver and could make a sign."

Jessica and Feston were caught in a time between days of constant activity behind them and a completed lodge in front where for the moment they just wanted to stop and rest. A slight breeze sent waves to break along the sand, forming a whispering song. It provided a steady background to other additions such as cries of gulls or rustling of palm fronds. Cardinals sang from moss-draped branches of live oaks or long leaf pines. Although not as often as inland, varied melodies of mocking birds spoke from shaded, hidden places among foliage.

The spell of rest was broken days later, when Jack approached to ask, "Would you care to come over for a special meal?"

"Thank you," answered Jessica, before she entered the cabin and returned with a container of corn cakes along with biscuits accompanied by a bottle of home brew saved for such an occasion.

"Wonderful," exclaimed Jack when he saw the cakes and brew. "We should get started."

Walking toward the workers' tents Jessica and Feston saw a boar spitted over a fire. Men sat in the area. Some were on the sand while others rested on chairs.

"Brew could come first, Jack," said one of the men before drinks were passed around. Jack added to the supply.

Already in a celebration mood, the drinks added an extra glow to good humor. Conversation became sparse while people savored a bounty of food, drink and company.

Before the sun dropped from view, withdrawing colors from sky, water, and land, Feston walked to what seemed to be the front of the gathering and said, "I thank each one of you for building a lodge here with our central cabin and a string of others for visitors. You have secured together boards, nails and other items.

Your contribution, however, is much greater. You have put into these structures the mortar of your spirit—many combined into one. Your appreciated contribution does not turn away from but joins with the presence of the wilderness and this is the best part of the Sands Lodge."

"I'm not sure I follow all that," stated Jack, "anyway, I like it."

When a heron flew through the darkening sky and landed on a roof of one of the cabins, Jack exclaimed, "A sign of partnership."

Soon after the special pig roast, Jack and crew finished their work. They left but, as the heron and egret resting on roofs, people arrived, drawn to the cabins.

One evening, when the lodge was full, as it usually was, Feston and Jessica went for one of their long walks along the beach. As usually occurred, a breeze blew toward shore where waves crested then splashed on the sand, sending flows of water forward only to have them halt before tumbling back to be replaced by the next, forming a song where sea meets land. Within this sound, more restful than most others, the two lodge owners journeyed.

"A day is ending in color along with maybe the most peaceful and thought-provoking time," said Fes. "As the day, our time here is in a sunset. When the morning sun rises to spread golden light to brighten the path for next travelers, they won't be us. A time is coming for our children to take over the lodge. Visitors who are drawn—receive a call—to this place, will arrive and for short moments will gather spiritual fulfillment from this Florida home. Our time here leaves a better place for others who travel after us. We have accomplished what we came here to do. In the future others will discover that the roots we started are deep."

Chapter 4

The Cabin

Present Day

After finding the foundation of the Sands Lodge, Jake Sands crossed the inlet and started walking along the trail that would take him back to his car parked beside the cabin belonging to Roger Tomkins. As Jake followed the natural path through the landscape his thoughts gathered information he had acquired.

Since I found that picture in my attic, he recalled, *of my great grandparents, Jessica and Feston Sands, standing at the back of their Sands Lodge, I've been hooked like any fish on a line. Hooked and tied by this picture, I've journeyed back in time, interviewing all the people I've met. Getting some detailed information from the retired sea captain, Caleb Collins, I took his advice and located Roger Tomkins who lives at the site where Jessica and Feston Sands had a cabin before they moved to the coast and built Sands Lodge. First caught by a picture, I'm now drawn to the area of land where the lodge was constructed between the inlet of a fresh water stream and the Gulf. I would like to build a cabin on the site of the Sands Lodge. My thoughts got me lost during my journey to the foundation. I should be careful or I'll get lost again.*

Not able to completely focus on the route, ideas continued to divert Jake's attention. I'm going to try to buy the property where the foundation is located, he resolved. *There, as I've considered, I'll build a cabin. With a minimum mark on the wilderness, I'll put a basic road in from the west, a branch from the main route to Roger's cabin. There will be no need to build a bridge over the fresh water stream. To pay for such plans, I'll use all the money I have along with any I can get or borrow. As the saying relates, "Always aim high although you might lite low."*

When the residence came into view, Roger was working in his garden. At Jake's approach, Roger exclaimed, "Are you a ghost or a person?"

"Person I think—and hope," he answered, taking off the pack.

"You've been gone so long, I've been getting ready to search for you," said Roger. "I haven't rushed out searching because you planned to be away for possibly a long time and took camping equipment with you."

"As you had mentioned before, the route was so easy to follow I became careless and got lost," stated Jake. "I found my way again not through locating the path but by finding the wilderness I had previously never understood, entered or known. By losing I found. I realized the true nature of the wilderness. This was an enormous discovery of something often looked at before but suddenly for the first time actually seeing. Step by step, insight after discovery I realized the wilderness is a messenger of the Creator who I will, having met, always follow and seek. I had heard such ideas in the past along with relating thoughts or statements. Having become immersed in a landscape, I saw it for the first time up close, tree by rock, each bird or animal—all working in long-term harmony. With this new understanding, I now enjoy the wilderness and lost any desire to ever leave it. Strangely I became at home when I thought at first I was lost. I can now stay with the landscape and live in a cabin I'm going to build on the foundation of the Sands Lodge, built by my great grandparents, Jessica and Feston Sands. I'll put a lane in from the west and won't have to build a bridge over the inlet."

"You have traveled a long way—further in knowledge than by trail," observed Roger. "Others have tried to buy that land—including me. The Seminoles own it and they won't sell. Everyone who sees that property so ideally situated between inlet and Gulf has thought of buying it. All fail. I've tried to purchase it—others have—and the answer is always the same. We don't even get close to an individual who specifically owns or controls ownership of the property. The Seminoles own that land. Because of the experience they have had, there is a wall present now."

"Do you know how I could visit the Seminoles?" asked Jake

"Drive to the Miccosukee community and ask for Calley Stonebear," answered Roger. "Other buyers have tried and they couldn't even get to see her. The land is not for sale."

"Not encouraging news," noted Jake. "Thanks for letting me park my car on your property. I think I'll leave from here and drive directly to see Calley Stonebear."

"I have to respect people who try the impossible," said Roger. "For your journey I'll get you a bag of oranges. Could I also get you coffee and sandwiches to get you started for your journey?"

"That would be appreciated," he replied.

"Sit down in the shade and I'll be right back," suggested Roger before he hastened into his cabin. In a short time he returned with a tray of food in addition to carrying a bag of oranges. He placed the tray on a table between his usual place under the live oak and the chair where Jake sat.

Enjoying the food and drink silently at first, Jake observed, "I hope I can make up for all the losses of my past. If life is a journey and we are all moving onward, although few know where, then I started my adventure poorly. I used to look at life as an ordeal to try to cope with or survive. In more recent years, I've changed to see not constant problems but overriding opportunities. When rain kept me inside and I went to the attic to check items stored there and found a picture of Jessica and Feston Sands standing in front of their lodge, I could have seen a struggle from the past that had no interest to me. According to my new outlook on life, I saw the picture as an opportunity. Some events in the past must be left there because they are signs of failure, not to be remembered or repeated. However there are accomplishments in the past that can always be celebrated and drawn upon for enlightenment that would help people in the future to enjoy enriched lives. Good advice and examples should be saved.

After seeing an opportunity, I've tried to find the lodge and the search itself has been an opportunity to meet an assortment of people. A most interesting character was the sea captain, Caleb Collins. He is a person who had a successful life because he did the work that called to him. He accepted the opportunity of life with the sea. It was a world he willfully entered then it took him to itself, showing life beyond his initial hopes or dreams. He never left the sea. Retirement to him only meant spending more time on shore physically while his spirit remained at sea."

Turning to look more directly at Roger, Jake said, "You are another interesting character. You walk your own trail becoming an original example. You determined you needed more peace and quiet. The search brought you here to the site of Jessica and Feston Sands' cabin. Our stories join here. Maybe we will continue to be neighbors."

"As I mentioned," replied Roger, "I tried to buy the land between the inlet and Gulf. Other people have also tried. I have discovered that when the Seminoles don't want to do something, they are serious about any such opinion. They seem to think in definite terms like the colors of their clothing. They are purely definite without blends."

Florida

Nodding toward the empty sandwich plate, Roger asked, "Like some more sandwiches?"

"No," he answered. "But thank you for asking. That's enough coffee too and both were appreciated. Maybe time to start traveling. Thank you also for the oranges."

When Jake was in his car, about to leave, Roger recalled, "A very attractive hiker, Cynthia, or just Cindy, Terrance, parks her car here and walks the trail as you and others do. She said she met a wild man who didn't wear clothes. Did that sighting have anything to do with you?"

"We all have our moments," laughed Jake.

"Some are stranger than others," countered Roger.

"I saw her twice," explained Jake. "The first time I had my clothes off to wash them. The second time I was carrying my clothes to keep them dry as I was crossing the inlet. I might have created a bad first impression."

"I hope you're more impressive when visiting the Miccosukee community," said Roger, smiling brightly.

"I like to always leave room for improvement," Jake replied.

"Traveling the trail to the Gulf was easy compared to the journey you are now starting," concluded Roger before Jake started the car.

"If I'm half as successful as you've been helpful I'll be your new neighbor," observed Jake.

"Only the believers achieve anything," said Roger and Jake's journey started. As the vehicle moved out of the laneway, Roger and his cabin almost immediately became hidden by foliage.

Not ready to leave the life he had discovered behind enveloping greenery, Jake thought, *walking the trail to the Gulf took me so much further than just to the water. I saw and was invited into the wilderness. Entering this world, I saw it for the first time, being a place where each part was connected. Encompassing vegetation jumped—moved—so filled it was with spiritual presence and light. Amazing too was to see this realm actually connected with me. I was part of it as likely each person is; however, we think people are industrious if they scoop away the wilderness to look for oil or take logs while leaving the remnant parts behind, disconnected to die. For the first time I understood the wild, realizing why people seek it for peace, comfort and solace to find relief from the hectic struggle of life. I saw the Creator's presence in the connection with each part while also joining people. People have awareness of such sacredness because wilderness is seen as a place where true rest and companionship can be found. The presence of the Creator in wilderness has constantly been reported by Indigenous people and lies at the heart of their protests to stop logging, fracking or mining that leaves behind incalculable devastation while taking away a small part for little profit. Seeing the wild for the first time, I realized I was not alone—and did not want to leave. While walking the trail I was looking for home. Off the trail, I thought at first I was lost then realized I was home. I had found what I had searched for since seeing the picture of Jessica and Feston Sands at the back of their lodge. I saw not just a picture of them but also a marker leading to my home. I have found it. Now to enjoy it I will try to build a cabin. Fist however I have to buy the land. Not often did the first newcomers to the Americas ever jump off the boats and pay for the land to be used. They thought the land was so free they had even discovered it. Even today truth of land is not understood. It is valuable beyond measurement and not only was it not lying vacant ready to be discovered by the newcomers but people had lived on this land for countless thousands of years. The land was not understood. The first people to live on it even today are just being discovered. The Conquistadors arrived in the Americas, destroyed people who had advanced cultures with cities including hospitals and libraries. On top of these ruins the invaders built churches as if such destroyers could possibly bring the Creator with them—a Creator representing love, kindness, compassion and forgiveness. The Creator was already in the Americas but the invaders could not see.*

Jake left his thoughts to one-handedly peel an orange Roger had given him. The juice restored his energy, dispelling any fatigue. *Now I see the importance of wilderness*, he concluded. *There I have found home. I would like to buy a corner of it where Jessica and Feston lived.*

Sunlight filled the car and surrounding landscape, bringing warmth everywhere. All car windows were down to let air blow inside from the seemingly endless vista of grass and sky. The air conditioner also added refreshing currents of coolness. The entire landscape seemed at first to be motionless except for a heron moving anciently across the sky.

So much of life is deceptive, reflected Jake. *This sea of grass seems to be static with nothing happening. Actually the area is a grass-covered sea of slowly moving fresh water. Life here is teeming, as it is ancient, with some new additions like pythons.*

Taken from his thoughts by the car bumping over something, Jake looked back and saw he had hit a large rattlesnake. It was turning over and twisting on the road then a second car went over the creature.

A few people are fishing along the roadside, observed Jake. *A fellow up ahead has something large on so maybe I could take a break and see what he is catching.*

Leaving the car at the side of the road, Jake walked toward a man wearing a vest topping light green trousers. A wide-brimmed hat shaded his face where there was revealed a person who enjoyed an easy life.

The water was deeper than expected and the fish was struggling powerfully. "I think it must be a good bass," said the guy to Jake. "I've caught them here before. It's starting to tire. We should see it soon."

The fish approached the shore where the fisherman was about to net the catch when there was an explosion as large jaws sent water splashing in all directions before teeth came down on the fish. The alligator swung its head from side to side before submerging, leaving behind a fisherman watching his broken line drift in the breeze.

"Some people will tell you there's nothin' out here," said the man while he caught the end of the line. "Actually, there's too much around. The place is full of life and not all if it is friendly. The only way to enjoy the area is to know it then the whole scene becomes magnificent. You have to be aware of all the parts—not just some of the rougher aspects."

"You sound like someone who has lived here a long time," replied Jake.

"All my life," answered the guy. "My family got into the real estate business early, buying low and selling high. I'm enjoying the profits. I fish for largemouth bass in the daytime and catfish at night. Today is the first time for feeding alligators."

"If you fall in I hope the alligators remember what a generous guy you are," added Jake before he started walking to his car. Calling back to the man, Jake said, "Thanks for the fishing show. You should keep some of those big bass for yourself."

Driving again along the road called Alligator Alley, Jake was surprised to see so many of the creatures resting in sunlight camouflaging the fact they could outrun most of those who watched the ridged reptiles and considered them to not be dangerous.

Reaching the Miccosukee community, Jake parked in front of a visitor center. He entered the building and saw a woman who was working behind a counter. Her clothing was colorful. Her face shone with beauty more attractive than any clothing or the turtle ornament in her long, black hair. Sunlight revealed her eyes to be almond brown although at first glance Jake thought they were black. She wore no makeup and likely knew she did not need it.

"Welcome to our center," she said pleasantly. "We have rides, programs, tours and restaurant available."

"I was wondering," replied Jake, "if I could talk to Calley Stonebear?"

She just looked at him without answering—so he continued, "I would like to talk to her about buying land she owns. It is the area between the fresh water inlet and the Gulf. The land is reached by a trail from Roger Tomkins' cabin."

"No," said the woman. "We have many programs, however, for your interest."

"Is there any chance of seeing Calley Stonebear?" he asked again.

"No," she replied before returning to some notes she was preparing when Jake entered the building.

"What is your name?" Jake asked, wanting to open some door—any door but the one he just saw close.

"Sally," she answered without looking up.

"I'm lucky and pleased to meet you," added Jake, continuing to try for any response other than the one he was getting. "Across the highway, are they taking people on airboat rides?"

"Yes," she replied.

"I'll try that," said Jake before walking to the door. He opened it, stepped outside and re-entered a warm, sun-lit world stirred by a refreshing breeze.

He crossed the road and approached a woman who was standing outside of a mobile office. She was wearing similarly colorful clothing like the woman at the center yet this person lacked much of the other's facial beauty. She was talking on a phone and looked up at Jake's approach. However, the phone conversation did not stop. A short distance away, a man stood beside a truck. Farther back, there was a dock where airboats were tied—ready for passengers.

Jake waited. Yet the phone conversation continued. When he started walking toward the man by the truck this fellow stepped inside the vehicle, closed the door and seemed to have put up a wall, ending any possibility for conversation.

Turning back to check the phone conversation, Jake read this message also. *Obviously,* he decided, *something has happened and they're not in a mood for rides or don't like taking just one person. They don't want to do rides and clearly that door is closed.*

Crossing the street, Jake entered the center again and approached Sally who continued to work behind the counter. "They don't want to take people on rides today," he reported.

"Our restaurant is open," said Sally showing no reaction to what seemed to be an unusual situation of people set up for rides but not carrying through with them.

I'm not ready for a restaurant, thought Jake. *I'm not ready to quit but others here are in their own ways telling me to stop trying to enter where I'm not welcome.* As a last possibility to at least keep a conversation going, he said, "At any rate, I'm pleased to meet you. My name is Jake Sands."

For the first time, she looked him right in the eyes and asked, "Sands?"

"Yes," he answered.

"Is your family from around here?" she continued.

"Yes," he said.

"Where did they live?" she asked.

"My great grandparents were Jessica and Feston Sands and they built a lodge beside the Gulf on land occupied by agreement with a Seminole family."

Sally picked up the phone and made a call. To the person she contacted, she said, "A man is here who would like to talk to you. His name is Jake Sands and he is interested in buying land previously occupied by the Sands Lodge." After a pause, she said, "OK." Making a second call, she said, "We need a ride for Jake Sands. He will meet you at the dock."

Looking at Jake directly, Sally said, "Go to the dock across the road. Charlie Cypress will take you to see Calley Stonebear."

"Wow," he exclaimed. "You are a lady of surprises."

"You are a man of surprises," she said, smiling.

"What changed your answers?" he asked.

"A lot of people have asked the questions you asked," she replied. "You are the first person to ask who is also called Sands."

"Should I ask why that name has magic?" he inquired.

"You are about to find out," she replied. "Charlie is waiting across the road at the dock. He does the airboat rides. I'll call him back and tell him of your destination."

"Thank you," exclaimed Jake who was being caught by a wave of excitement, having gone from slammed doors to acceptance beyond his wildest hopes or dreams.

When he was leaving, Sally said, "Welcome to our home."

After walking to the dock, Jake saw the same man who had been at the truck. His jeans and colorful shirt were loose fitting, adding casualness to his calm manner. Straight hair bordered the man's round face where eyes watched Jake closely.

"Your name?" was all that was said.

"Jake Sands," he replied. "You're Charlie?"

"Yes," he answered. "Put on these ear plugs," he directed, extending to Jake the plugs. Accepting them, and before they were put into place, Charlie continued, "The ride is ready. Let's get traveling."

When both men were sitting, the motor started with a loud blast and soon the craft was speeding through a world where a straight horizon divided colors of green below and blue above. The rush of air was refreshing during the day's heat. Compared to the boat's speed, a heron seemed to be more of a silhouette against the sky rather than anything that was actually flying. Sawgrass prairie extended to the horizon where it was broken only by low islands. Distance offered no variety of color although at close range variations depicted changes in depth of water. Generally however the land seemed as endless as the sky and the two realms might have appeared to be blended together except for the presence of the dividing line of horizon.

Jake was settling in to accepting a long journey when high ground appeared. The boat approached a dock, came along beside it and Charlie said, "Calley is expecting you."

Jake stepped onto the dock. He turned to thank Charlie for the ride but could only wave when the motor blasted, sending the craft back into full speed.

He stopped for a moment to slow down what was happening and look around at his present circumstances. There was a river of flowing water everywhere. Sawgrass added green hues to reach the sky where a flock of egrets flashed white colors against the greenish blue background. *I'm on an island*, reflected Jake. *I have no way back. Ahead there is a path leading to a sprawling house with a screened veranda.*

He walked along the dock, approached the veranda's front door and heard a woman's voice say, "Come in."

He entered a long, winding porch where refreshing outside breezes entered bringing all the outside with them. *This building*, reflected Jake, *is not separate but part of the surrounding world.*

In the everglades freshness, stood a woman of similar beauty to Sally yet this person had some gray color mixing with the long, straight black hair bordering her slightly lined face. Dark brown eyes flashed when she said, "Welcome Jake Sands. Please sit down. I have lemonade and corn biscuits prepared. Glasses of beer are also ready to put you at rest while you tell me a story."

After sitting down, facing the border of screens that did not keep out but only slightly shaded the outside view, he said, "I have a hunch your story is much more interesting. You are Calley Stonebear?"

"Yes," she answered. "Relax. Try some corn biscuits and lemonade while you tell me what you say is a less interesting story."

"Thank you," he said before sampling a biscuit and then the lemonade. "Your hospitality is appreciated."

"We welcome friends," she replied. "What brings you here?"

"In the attic of my house," he explained, "I found an old photograph of my great grandparents, Jessica and Feston Sands. They were standing at the back of a building having a sign with the words, Sands Lodge. The people and the lodge were identified on the back of the photograph.

"Out of curiosity for this place and time, I traveled to the coast of Florida. My journey came to a cabin where Jessica and Feston had lived. The cabin has been rebuilt and is presently the home of Roger Tomkins. He directed me to follow a trail to the Gulf. Along this route, I got lost yet became found again by an acquaintance I had previously often seen but never understood. The stranger I met was the wilderness. After entering it, being in it, I, for the first time saw, recognized then realized I was part of this complicated yet indescribably beautiful realm. The landscape around me brightened, seemed to move, making me aware I was part of it and it was a connecting presence or messenger of the Creator. I'll never see the wilderness the same way again. Life itself for me has changed. We are not, nor could we ever be, alone and would be only if this was our choice. The Creator that I saw present through the wilderness was all love and kindness. I felt at home in the wild and lost all desire to leave it. Remaining there, I walked to the Gulf. Following a search, I located the foundation of Sands Lodge."

Having come to a conclusion of one part in his account, Jake stopped talking.

He sampled more of the amazingly delicious corn cakes, again sipped lemonade then looked around at his surroundings. The outside realm was in the veranda bringing the breeze laced by fragrances of a seemingly endless sawgrass prairie where all types of life found home.

"I heard," continued Jake, "you own this land. I was wondering if I could purchase this property? I would build a cabin on the old foundation and bring a laneway for a car in from the west so I wouldn't have to put a bridge across the inlet."

Calley walked toward Jake, took away his empty lemonade glass. She went into a back room and returned to bring two large glasses filled with beer.

"Thank you," he said, receiving the glass. Its sides were already moist from warmth of the day.

He enjoyed a long sample of the refreshing drink while Calley sat, sipping from her glass, put it down then looked outside as a heron dropped from the sky and started stalking shallows by the dock.

Continuing to look at the sawgrass river, the elegant lady, said, "Jake Sands, the answer to your question is no, you can not buy this property that has been home to so many for so long."

Jake felt the brightness of surrounding light fade as a gray film settled over his view. He fought this reaction and strove to listen more intently to this woman. *Appearances are deceptive*, he warned himself. *This is the everglades and like it there is so much more happening here than is seen on the surface. This woman's presence holds my attention. Her voice draws me into a time, realm and culture that are full of the past, present and above all, this land.*

"Thank you for your wonderful refreshments and hospitality. Everything is most welcoming—except your answer. Your answer is no?" he said.

"That's right," she replied, smiling.

Jake enjoyed a long sip of the cool, refreshing drink before the woman tried a similar sample.

A trace of worry coursed through Jake when the woman looked directly at him and held her gaze. "The answer is no," she repeated. "You can't buy something you already own."

Jake choked on beer he had just about swallowed. After regaining some composure, he asked, "Already own?"

"Yes," she said, smiling.

"I've been intrigued ever since I saw that photograph of two people standing at the back of Sands Lodge," he exclaimed. "I've never been as interested as now."

"Time for me to tell you a story," she said.

"Your story seems to be much more interesting than mine," declared Jake. He gazed at this attractive woman surrounded by screens on a porch where the everglades entered and were part of the home. Colors of blue and green predominated in the outside realm. Inside, Jake waited for the speaker who was in no hurry. As in the world of flowing water and sawgrass, where time seemed to not matter, there was the same deep restfulness of timelessness within this home.

While looking out toward the dock where the heron was standing with wings spread, catching drying rays of sunlight, Calley said, "What people see along the highway is for tourists. We must get to know each other so we can stop being strangers. Like the surface of the everglades however, there is so much more underneath. The Miccosukee or Seminole community today is a modern world enterprise with numerous businesses all set in law. Among many other ventures we produce our own food, including cattle ranches. We supply our community and the rest of society. Gone are the days when the wilderness could provide. Today the wilderness is our joy, life and church where we walk with the Creator.

The Europeans—newcomers—said we had to get rid of our old cultures and languages in order to have a modern life. We are now correcting such mistakes. Around the world, people of different nations have kept their ancient cultures and are all leading modern lives. Like the others today, we are keeping our traditional cultures including languages and we are leading modern lives. People often wonder what is happening in Indian country everywhere. The answer is we are working with the law and maintaining our traditions while living modern lives. If people ask you what I told you that rocked your boat such can be your reply. That is what's happening with Indian Nations throughout all of the Americas. Such is the present and the future.

When the Europeans—the newcomers—arrived, they used the law against us. We know the importance of law. We have always had law and kept records."

Outside by the dock, the heron flew to a shallow area, stood motionlessly just before the neck and head shot forward. Straitening, the bird held in its beak, a slender fish. With a quick flip of the beak the fish, head first, started down the long neck. The neck straightened up once before the heron shook with satisfaction of obtaining a fine meal. Hunting resumed, not because the hunter was now hungry but because this was life.

Turning to look directly at Jake, and with fire in her eyes freshly stoked, she stated, "We know the importance of law and land. Jessica and Feston Sands might be the first newcomers who paid for land they received. We have always kept records. The transactions for that property are remembered."

Jake finished the beer almost in an attempt to prepare for what this day might be bringing. He saw the everglades stirring with life both outside and inside the veranda. And this woman, whom he just met but felt he knew, seemed to be coming to something definitely affecting him. "Jake Sands, you can't buy that land because you already own it. You can't pay for it because Jessica and Feston Sands have already paid. Sally, who you have met is one of our lawyers. She will be arriving here and bringing the deed. Also, there will be stated if the Sands family ends use of the land then it goes back to the only other owner it has and that is the Miccosukee or Seminole community."

Calley left to get refills of beer. Jake rushed to the washroom. When he came back, he enjoyed the new refreshment. It relaxed him, enabling the possibility to fully enjoy what he was hearing. He caught the spirit of the community, as the people saw their lives and lived together with, not against, the environment.

"If all people," he said, were as just as you, I can only begin to imagine the prosperity we would all be enjoying and the richness of lives. Life is hard, even intended to be that way, but through our own choices we too often turn hardship into tragedy."

"If all people were as just as your family," answered Calley, we could have saved great civilizations of the Americas."

Cries of turns coming from outside brought attention to these birds diving for minnows splashing at the surface where they must have been driven by fish feeding below. "The first people," continued the woman with a voice that was soft, yet had a ring to it, making each word clearly heard, "known to have called the land you are interested in home were the Timucuans. They lived there longer than records have been kept. That's actually south of their usual territory as most southwestern Florida was home of the Calusa.

When the Spaniards arrived, they treated Indigenous nations brutally, also spreading new diseases that killed more people than the number who remained. The Spanish ransacked cities including libraries and hospitals where medical people might have been able to develop cures for the new diseases. Most likely those conquistadors who spread diseases also prevented their cures. The loss or reduction of Indigenous culture is a tragedy and this was often done intentionally. Researchers today have not discovered a single use for plants from the Americas that was not previously known by Indian nations. These early developers have supplied over half of the present world's food supply. Nations near mountains to the south built cities using stone. Many of these structures remain, leaving markers of cities that had been there. Farther inland, societies built with earth and wood. Over time, little that was built has survived. Today contour mapping is revealing the presence of what were great cities.

In Florida, remnants of the first inhabitants including the Calusa and Timucua joined members of the Creek nation who were journeying southward. Today we are known often as Seminoles.

The land of your interest was first home of the Timucuans then Seminoles. Jessica and Feston Sands built a cabin then a lodge with the approval of Seminoles, particularly one family—Ray and Orchid Stonebear, my ancestors.

Jessica and Feston Sands uncovered gold, which had been buried with haste by a retreating group of Spaniards. This gold had been looted from Indigenous nations farther south. Jessica and Feston shared their discovery with Ray and Orchid

Stonebear—on behalf of the Seminoles. Records have been kept. I am the keeper of records. Through long occupancy, the Timucuans and Seminoles own the land, including the Sands Lodge. By sharing gold, Jessica and Feston have also obtained ownership of this area. Only these two groups can own that land. After the time of the Stonebear family, another Seminole family will continue my position. The Sands claim has come to you.

You, Jake Sands, have legal claim to the land and payment has already been made. There is some signing for you to do and a deed is on its way here—now."

With the background of the everglades and its fresh breeze moving softly through the screened veranda, Jake had listened to Calley's story. Her words had caught him. He traveled with them through time from the past to the present and suddenly he was directly involved. Almost in disbelief of what he had heard, he said, "I'm getting a deed to the property for no further cost?"

"Yes," she answered.

"Is there any concern about my plan to build a laneway and cabin?"

"The area is yours," she confirmed. "Regarding value, we think the most valuable land in the world is wilderness."

"Yes," exclaimed Jake. "What a joy to hear you say that. I learned, recently, this message by getting lost along the trail."

"When you told me what had happened to you during your walk," replied Calley, "I knew I was meeting the true owner of that piece of property."

The sound of an airboat arriving grew louder then suddenly stopped. Shortly afterward, Sally from the tourist center entered the home where Calley greeted her and said, "Thank you for your work—and so quickly done."

To Jake, Sally said, "We meet again." Taking documents from an envelope, she explained, "The deed is ready for signing."

"Well done, Sally," replied Calley. "Some beer or lemonade?"

"Your lemonade is the best," she answered, before Calley brought her some and Sally sat beside a table where she placed the documents.

To Jake, Calley explained, "Sally is a lawyer and also does real estate. She looks after the Sands-Stonebear property.

Signatures make the land yours. You have a Florida home."

Sally said, "Charlie is ready to take Jake back."

When offered, Jake read over the deed along with related material. Finding the printed words to outline what he had heard, he added his signature, received a copy then turned to the two women and said, "Such an adventure is in a realm I will try to understand. This entire occurrence is my stepping or riding into a world, or aspect of it, that is like a dream happening to me while I'm awake. Maybe that's what the spiritual side is about. We find ourselves in the best of situations in actual life rather than just through dreaming. There is justice here beyond what we often see in life."

"The good in people far outweighs the evil done by a few individuals who have chosen to turn away from the Creator," replied Calley. "Most people don't turn away."

"How can I ever thank you?" he asked.

"Welcome home," answered Calley. "That's all this is. You have returned."

"Before coming here," said Jake, "I was told you won't see people and the land is not for sale."

"What you heard then is true," she related. "I don't meet outsiders—nor do any of us."

"The good of life maybe should become better known by outsiders—so there would no longer be any," suggested Jake.

"Such a day will come," Calley replied. "That's a purpose of our cultural centers. The trail from the past is far reaching. The journey ahead is just as long."

Looking at Calley, Sally said, "Your lemonade is always appreciated."

"So is your work," repeated Calley.

"Time to see Charlie?" asked Sally.

"Yes," she answered. "I'll take him some lemonade."

"Wonderful to meet you both," said Jake to the women before they all went outside. "A whole new world has opened. I hope in the future others will meet the people I have visited today."

"Welcome home, Jake," replied Calley while they walked amid sunshine and a slight breeze. Grass rippled like waves on the ocean. Clouds moved slowly across a seemingly endless sky.

Charlie had been using a cast net to catch minnows for the heron and an egret. He put away the net and thanked Calley for the glass of lemonade. "Calley's best," he exclaimed, after returning the glass.

"You work quickly," Jake said to Sally while they prepared to put on earplugs.

"Land concerns are kept up to date and ready for immediate action," she replied. "Traditionally we thought long-standing occupation of land was proof of ownership. Like all cultures, we want to keep our traditions while living in the modern world. To do this we need bilingual ways of life. In other words, today we use the paper system to prove land title."

Florida

When the three people were settled in the boat, they waved back to Calley just before the craft, motor roaring, swirled away from the dock and at full speed started to move across the sawgrass prairie. In a short time, the return trip was completed. Stepping out of the airboat, Jake said, "Thanks Charlie."

"Welcome Jake Sands," he replied then Sally and Jake crossed the road. Beside his car, Jake said, "One day this is a strange place in a sea of grass. In a short time I realize I have friends and discover I'm almost part of the family."

"Not almost, Jake," she replied, smiling beautifully. "The Sands are part of our traditions."

"Thank you for your help," he replied.

"These records guarantee on paper our lives," she said then started walking back to the center.

"Good deeds have long lives," he added before getting into his car and starting the motor. He turned westward to retrace his route after leaving Roger Tomkins' cabin.

When I began this journey, he recalled, *I had only a photograph of my great grandparents standing at the back of Sands Lodge. People arriving by car might consider the first part of the lodge to come into view as the front but actually this side faced the Gulf. Now, as I drive toward Roger's cabin, I not only have a picture but I've entered it. I'm there. I'm in my Florida home. We never know what lies around the corner or what might happen from one day to the next. I'm not just a visitor or a seeker of the past for I live here. I'll not be repeating life because I'll be reacting to it in my uniqueness and making my own choices. They will determine my success or failure. Opportunity is what life is. I wish I could have known this a long time ago when my days were beginning. I would have seen life as an opportunity to be enjoyed rather than just one difficulty after another to be met, coped with or sometimes just survived.*

Seeing the same fisherman who previously had lost a bass to an alligator, Jake turned off the highway and parked beside the other person's vehicle. Seeing Jake, the man held up a fish, much the same size as the one lost. With a wide smile brightening the fellow's face, he exclaimed, "Life is good."

"Nice catch," replied Jake, as he welcomed the refreshing breeze blowing in from vast spaces of grass and sky. "Do you work in real estate or just your family?"

"My family got here early," he replied. "They bought up land, kept it for a while then sold, making a fortune. I've inherited what I have. I look after the fishing now—some tennis and mainly golf."

"You and the alligator are dining well today," concluded Jake, as he got back inside his car. The other guy did the same and Jake waited for him to drive away before returning to the journey.

Troubled by a tumult of thoughts, Jake turned off the road again. He got out of the car, sat on a cross piece of a bridge.

Below him, water flowed clearly. Minnows rested in the stream.

Who could believe, he wondered, *that life on earth happened by some cosmic accident? How many accident processes would have to occur to get a group of minnows swimming together, comfortable with each other's company, in fresh water of a shallow river miles wide and flowing to the sea?*

A breeze rippling the sawgrass brought freshness to warmth. *That guy who caught the bass inherited what he has,* recalled Jake. *I've inherited my holdings. I thought less of that guy because he did not work for his wealth. His fortune likely came from injustice. Mine has come because of justice. This discredit and credit belongs to people of the past. He took his income as a chance to do nothing. I know I so far have done nothing. The difference here lies in the fact I am just starting. I cannot follow the trail of others, nor can they follow mine. We each have our own journey to take, each one forming original choices, making all of life new. When things are running smoothly like now, I see a plan to life and the presence of spirit—the Creator. When trouble comes, I lose sight of the plan and the Creator. I must try to fix this mistake. I have to remember when I can't see the presence of help this is the time when I have to have faith. Such is the journey I've set. I must now stay on course.*

Returning to driving, Jake was surprised again by the number of alligators basking in sunlight at the side of the road, next to the water. Roger's lane came into view. *Shadows are lengthening marking the close of this day,* noted Jake. *I can't stay here long because I have much work to do.*

"I told you so," said Roger; as Jake stepped out of the car. "You can't buy that land. Will you have some coffee?"

"Yes, thank you," answered Jake, before he sat on the same chair he had left hours ago.

Roger entered his cabin. He returned carrying two cups of steaming drink. After giving one to Jake, he sat on the other chair.

"Good to make plans and have dreams," said the bearded man. His hair was not only naturally white or gray, yet bleached further by the sun. "That's what you had and they will remain that way. Others have tried—had the same dream— and failed to have it come true. As I have mentioned previously, I also planned—tried—to move to the Gulf shore."

"Good coffee, by the way," observed Jake. "Good because I didn't have to make it and also a richly flavored blend I really enjoy."

Another sip later, Jake recalled, "You have a cabin built on the foundation started by my great grandparents, Jessica and Feston Sands. I plan to build a cabin on the foundation of the Sands Lodge. Like you did, I'm going to put a lane in from the west."

Roger stared, wondering why Jake was continuing down this road. "I've been telling you, that's not possible," he said.

"And you're right—absolutely right in saying I can't buy that land," replied Jake, enjoying the moment.

"Why then are you continuing to build these dreams?" asked Roger.

"I can't buy the land because I was told I already own it," explained Jake, before giving Roger the deed and other papers.

Roger took the papers and read them, gazing in disbelief and finishing with the world he now saw in a different way. He could only stare while the impossible faded to be replaced by the most incredible set of facts he had ever heard. "I see how things are," he whispered. "But how did all this happen?"

Jake told him the story behind the papers. When the words ended, Roger said, "I'm pleased—maybe honored—to be at least in a small way part of such wonderful events. It's like actions of kindness and consideration being thrown into a calm lake of life and ripples of resulting kindness and consideration expanding outward through generations. You, Jake, are like a bridge providing a path of better ways between the Seminoles and more recent settlers."

"I'm pleased to have you as a neighbor and part of the story," replied Jake.

"Part of the story," repeated Roger as he stood up.

"That's a place I want to be," he stated. "I'll be back." He walked again to the cabin and entered it, soon returning carrying two tall glasses of beer. "I know you are driving," he said, giving Jake one glass. "We'll just have one but a celebration is in order. I have to make one more trip into the kitchen." Leaving again, he came back carrying two plates. Each one was topped with a sandwich. After sliding one plate to Jake's side of the table, he explained, "I didn't make the ham although I did shoot and roast it. The bread though is home made. It is one of the few things I cook along with biscuits. I grow the onions and peppers in addition to cucumbers to make pickles. Have to buy the dill, garlic, vinegar and salt. Homemade pickles are a specialty and so is the chili sauce. For it, I grow the tomatoes, onions and peppers. I have to buy the celery, salt, cinnamon, brown sugar and vinegar. So for your sandwich, you have homemade pickles, chili sauce, garden onions and home shot ham with mustard on the side. Many people like mustard with ham. That's what we can call a celebration sandwich."

Giving Jake papers, Roger continued to say, "These are my recipes for making bread, pickles and chili sauce."

"What a wildly wonderful harvest," exclaimed Jake. "Do I have your approval to grow these items and make this amazing sandwich?"

"Of course," he replied. "As I mentioned before, it's going to be called the celebration sandwich."

After tasting a pile of food stacked on the plate and trying the refreshing beer, Jake said, "Taste matches the looks. Thank you. The service here is great topped only by the wonderful food and drinks."

"Not every day do I get a new outlook on life like you have shown me today," explained Roger. "That trail to the Gulf has led to many interesting stories. Your account tops them all."

"I appreciate you not minding having me copy this wildly wonderful invention called a sandwich," exclaimed Jake. "But you know from now on I have to stop copying other people and tell my own story."

After sipping some of the drink, Roger looked directly at Jake, and stated, "The best part of all I've heard today occurred when you told me I was included in the story. Well I have news for you. You are connected in your own way, making unique decisions. I am and you are too."

"That's the part I must not overlook again because this is the message I learned when I got lost along the trail—everything is connected," explained Jake. "I have been walking my own trail, telling—living—my own story. It's part of a larger forest of trees, people and all life. I am being true to my own, original life."

Roger rekindled the fire. After finishing this routine, he sat down again and said, "I came to this cabin to get away from the fray where I was busy doing things and not really thinking about why I was working on them. With all the noise and rushing cleared away, I found time to discover the joy of getting up in the morning and being free to decide what to do—without rushing. There was new opportunity to enjoy the first light of day and the life it stirred, bringing into view again all the forms and shapes some of us can not see in the dark. I had time to enjoy the birds along with animals and watch them carrying out intelligent lives. Most of all, I could consider not only what I was doing but also, most essentially, what I should be doing. You have just told me I'm part of a larger event—connected to the best side of life; and the good side is spiritual. You have become aware of being in the presence of the Creator. I know this presence is real because of being included in your story. The next step for me is to experience the presence. Life is spiritual. In the background of my thoughts I knew this and for such a reason I came here. Now I see more clearly my purpose and the trail to follow. It's all spiritual."

"Who would you recommend as builders of a cabin and a lane?" asked Jake.

"The same people who built my place," he answered. "The manager's name is Will Jenkins.

"Would you please call him and tell him I'll be coming in to see him?"

"I'll call after your visit," Roger replied.

"That is now," said Jake because I have much to do before this day ends."

"I enjoy your wonderful story and being included in it," said Roger as Jake stood up.

"Thank you for your exceptional hospitality and making that call," said Jake.

Roger wrote the builder's name and address on some paper then added a sketch showing how to get to this business. After providing the paper, he said, "This information will get you started."

"Wonderful events are unfolding," exclaimed Jake, "and thank you for your help."

Roger followed Jake to his car. He got inside and started the motor. Speaking through the open window, Roger said, "Thanks for making me a believer that the impossible can be accomplished."

Jake drove along the lane then turned westward toward last colors of the setting sun. Into a landscape painted many shades of red, he traveled until he came to the address Roger had written on paper.

Seeing a tall man talking to other people in front of a building that was closed for the night, Jake drove beside him and asked, "Are you Will Jenkins? I'm Jake Sands."

To Jake, the man said, "Park your car." To the other men, he explained, "I have to talk to this guy. I'll see you in the morning."

After Jake parked his vehicle and stepped out, the tall fellow approached him and said, "I'm Will Jenkins. Come on inside."

Jake followed the fellow as he walked back to the building then opened a side door. They proceeded to an office that was cluttered not to the point of sloppiness yet just seeming to be a place where much activity was taking place.

Will sat down on a large oak chair facing a desk. Jake took one of three chairs on the opposite side.

"Roger called me and told me your story," said Will. "It's so fantastic I was just telling the other men. You'll be famous around here for being the guy who did the impossible and got the Seminoles to sell not just any land but the area so many others have tried to buy. And you got it for no charge. Now there's a story that will spread."

Will was a large man who seemed to portray strength in all his features from muscles pushing against his shirt to roughness of his face. He gave the impression of a person who lived on work from dawn till dusk and would be uncomfortable in any other situation. If he wore a suit, it would not conceal the fact the man that the clothes covered did not fit either them or any situation where they were required. "What do you want us to do?" he asked.

"Put a lane in from the west to the foundation of the Sands Lodge," answered Jake. "Also build a cabin on the foundation."

"We first set up a tent camp with all living accommodations including wooden outhouses at the back," explained Will. "Later they become tool sheds. We would start a lane at the same time as the cabin. I know the plan well. We were about to work on similar projects in the past until the property approval always failed. I tried this same idea myself. Being a practical guy, I thought everything had a price until I tried buying that property. You are a legend in your own time."

"I have to give credit to my great grandparents who had a lodge on that property and they were considerate of their neighbors," recalled Jake. "Sometimes a little kindness we do that we think is unseen actually sinks deep roots and spreads out through many generations. With regard to our building program, I'll set up a tent camp beside yours and also travel at first by boat."

"We could start tomorrow," said Will.

"I hoped you would say that," replied Jake. "Since this project happened, I've felt in a hurry, as if I'm late for something. Maybe I'm in a rush to get going with the rest of my life."

"That's how I operate," exclaimed the large man. "We're going to get along just fine." Standing, he added, "I'll go and see the other foreman now so he and I can both start getting the men and supplies ready."

"Fortunately I know when to take good advice," said Jake, after he also stood up. "Taking Roger's recommendation of you ensures success. We are going to have a great time."

"I enjoy being part of such a project and your story," said Will. They walked outside, got into their vehicles and started preparing for sunrise.

Jake rented a room at a resort. He kept windows open in order to hear waves crashing along the shore. This sound called out, filling him with a feeling of hearing his future. Here he was home. *I must never again*, he resolved, *be long away from the sea. Life for me lies within the sound of waves where there is also an almost constant breeze laced with a fragrance of salt and sometimes fish. As a change from being in a car for so long, I think I'll walk to a restaurant.*

Answering a call of the Gulf, he crossed the sand then started to walk quickly beside waves as they curled upward, crested and crashed into bubbling streams flowing along sand only to be drawn back to be replaced by the next wave. *This has been a life-changing day*, he recalled. *I'll have to make some phone calls to the north in order to sell my house and property. Contents will be stored. For occasions when I travel north again, I'll rent rooms. Right now I need to total my savings to cover upcoming expenses. I haven't discussed cost with Will. There are people I naturally trust and he's certainly one of them.*

Entering the restaurant, Jake was met by an aroma of grilled fish. He selected a chair next to a table providing a view of the Gulf. The moon was rising, sending a silver path along the water. *That silver trail*, reflected Jake, *reminds me again life for me must be where I can hear waves and catch a fragrance of salt from the almost constant breeze. Air above ocean carries freshness and gives to coastal Florida a flower-salt-fish scented fragrance so special a person if perceptive knows he or she has entered the boundaries of Florida without reference to any other sign.*

Continuing to watch the silver trail, Jake traveled with it, walking with his thoughts and was startled when he heard someone ask, "Anything to drink?"

Turning to see who had spoken, Jake saw an attractive woman who had blonde hair combed back away from her face where blue eyes saw him without apparent interest. *This woman sees too many customers to note them much as individuals,* he observed. *She does not and could not know my life is ablaze with a journey to follow beyond my previous wildest hopes and dreams.*

Noticing she was waiting impatiently for an answer, he said, "Draft please."

Florida

A tall, cold glass of refreshing drink arrived quickly, along with a menu.

Jake said, "Thank you and please add a grouper sandwich with cheese."

"OK," she replied, before leaving to place the order.

Jake enjoyed a long sample of the beer as he returned to let the path of light from the rising moon take his thoughts with it out to sea. *The journey of my life so far has brought me here to this restaurant and dreams sent out along silver-topped waves,* he mused. *Amazing to think a photograph found in my attic would have such an impact on my life. So far I think I have made the best choices because I know—feel—I'm on course and just where I should be at this time. Tomorrow I'll purchase equipment needed to set up a tent camp next to the tents of the workers.*

Like most land beside water there will already exist a trail following natural contours of land where a lane will be constructed. I'll check this route with Will in the morning. All possibilities are assembling together with harmony that occurs when a project is right and ready to happen. Some people call this sacred synchronism or things just taking place as they should even though sometimes bad, even terrible, events occur. Some days are so dark the light does not shine through although eventually it does. If we did not want to learn, develop through trouble, we would stay on the spiritual side, called heaven. I try to live above the fray and, most of the time, succeed. I deliberately don't remember them but I've had days that are so dark I can't see the light. I know that's when we have to have faith but even that occasionally if difficult to achieve. Fortunately these events don't come often. Today the light is here with me at this restaurant.

After almost finishing the draft, he recalled *I, at one time, thought sacred synchronism or the guided coming together of events was just a theory; however I've seen it unfold too often for such a process to be anything other than a real and almost constant occurrence. We often meet people at just the right time. I find a photograph and in it I see not the past but my future. Seeking the spiritual road is the only requirement to staying on it regardless of the worst obstacles that attack our progress.*

Jake was ready for a refill of the glass when the meal arrived. *Always the right food to order in a new restaurant,* he concluded, as he enjoyed the delicious sandwich. The woman returned and refilled the glass.

After the meal, he finished the drink just before the woman brought the bill. She dropped it on the table, was turning to leave when Jake asked, "Is this a career for you?"

"No," she replied, as her eyes sparkled with some deeper blue, showing interest for the first time. "I'm doing graduate work with fish. That's my specialty."

"Mine too," he said. "You have research. I have theories."

"I'm Tess Taber," she offered. "What's your name?"

"Jake Sands," he replied. "I'm building a cabin farther down the shore."

"I know the shoreline," she said. "Where is your cabin? And interesting to hear you say cabin because most people build mansions."

"The mansion is already there," he stated. "I'm just adding a cabin to have a place to stay."

"Couldn't you stay in the mansion?" she asked.

"My cabin is going to be in the mansion," he answered. "The mansion is the wilderness."

"Wow," she exclaimed. "That's the world as I know it. The sea is also a wilderness. I study it."

"I live in it," he added.

"Maybe you'll be back at this restaurant?" she inquired.

"Yes," he said, standing. "The sea has called both of us," he added before placing cash on the table to cover the bill and tip.

"Thank you," she exclaimed, noticing the large tip.

Jake walked along the sand, proceeding toward his room. He was suddenly weary. Seeing some dunes, he walked to them. Sounds of waves brought sleep.

In the morning, amid dawn's light, he walked to his room. He turned on some lights and they revealed compact areas where everything necessary was supplied with no extras. *This place is just right*, he noted. He settled in with a shower followed by breakfast. Lastly, he sat in the most comfortable chair after turning it so he could see life outside and watch early rays of sunshine greet the Gulf.

Sipping coffee, he reasoned, *I have a lot of planning to do along with preparations to get ready. Will knows the cabin site and can get started right away. We need a lane constructed to follow natural contours set out by a path that will already be there. Of particular interest is the cabin. It will have a propane fireplace in addition to an electric air conditioner. The lodge would have needed fresh water to be as clean as possible for drinking. Likely there is a spring. I'm quite sure during my longest walks I could reach the cabin site from here.*

Leaving the room, Jake started buying equipment and supplies required to set up his own tent camp next to the site prepared by the crew. *They will have a separate area with a fire for cooking*, he noted. *Each item, such as a tent that I'll need, I'll either take or have delivered to Will's construction office. All materials will be loaded onto the company's workboats and taken to the building area.*

After working late into the day, Jake concluded his preparations. Afterward, he left his car at the resort and walked to the restaurant.

Tess approached and asked, "Draft?"

"Yes, thanks," he answered.

She brought the drink, placed it on the table in front of him and said, "As I mentioned before, I'm doing research on the world of fish. How interested are you in fish?"

Florida

Jake looked out through the windows, seeing the Gulf where waves were crashing along the shore. "Are you interested in a long answer or will a short one do?"

"The restaurant is not busy," she replied. "I have as much time as you have interest."

"I walked in the wilderness of the land," he explained. "I got lost. By having nothing, I suddenly realized I had nothing only because I could not see what was around me. I was in a mansion greater than any built by people. I saw this realm for the first time. Suddenly it brightened and either actually jumped or just moved in my heightened awareness, when I realized everything was connected to each other part and also to me. I was amazed to see I was not separate because I had always felt that way. I was part of this indescribable wealth for it was rich with life. The connecting part was spiritual—the presence of the Creator. I was no longer lost. The sea, the Gulf, is also a wilderness like the land. Between the two wilds there is a border of sand. This is where I like to walk—where the wilderness of the sea meets the wildness of the land. Fish are a central part of the sea—the Gulf. If people take only what the sea can provide, we will always have this food. If too much is removed, the supply will be gone. We must always have respect. With the increased demand for food by more and more people, along with disrespectful harvesting, there is rapidly approaching the time when people must grow, ranch, farm, or otherwise produce all their food requirements rather than just taking from the wilderness. Wild areas themselves, through carelessness are being diminished. As I've mentioned, we must always have respect."

"You have increased my view of fish," observed Tess. "I knew parts of the sea are connected; yet you have explained the tie is greater than I thought—and it's spiritual."

"People hear about the sacred presence but seeing it changes everything," said Jake. "Actually believing the spiritual side is true makes life new and nothing is the same again. Regardless of the darkness that comes and the most difficult times, there is knowledge of a stronger spiritual presence eventually more noticeably present—if we will only stay on course and not turn away. We have to have faith. Sometimes that's the only buoy or lighthouse to guide the way as we sail the sea from one day, the next night and those that follow. Eventually the journey is beyond our wildest hopes and dreams."

"With respect we can take fish from the sea," noted Tess. "They also, more and more, are being farmed. Someday I plan to run a fish farm. I'm now qualified as a veterinarian. I work part time in a veterinary clinic just east from here—down the beach."

"You are almost too busy to work here," noted Jake.

"The restaurant helps to pay for my plans and this type of work is a holiday," she replied.

"I've discovered the wilderness is a messenger," observed Jake. "You have seen the same vastness. Maybe one part of the wild is enough for one person to explore."

"What kind of work are you doing?" she asked.

"My employment is accounting," he answered. "Now I'm building a cabin farther down the beach."

"I've forgotten that I'm supposed to be working here," she exclaimed. "As you said, however, I'm likely too busy to continue. While I'm here, should I order you a grouper sandwich?"

"Yes," he replied. "With cheese of course—and a refill."

Bringing first the refill of draft, Tess said, "You have given me an idea. You have altered the course the ship of my life is taking. I've been taking on too much. I'm no longer going to do research for fish and working here for holidays. I'm going to stop working here."

"Clearly I talk too much," said Jake.

"I needed the talk," she countered. "My study of fish has been just that—too much study. I'm going to leave that part and focus on being a veterinarian. I'll also return to being a fisherman—or should say fishing person."

"Wow," he exclaimed. "Maybe you should not have listened to me."

"You are right," she said. "All parts of the wild are too vast to see at once. I'm going to focus on the veterinary clinic—the wilderness of the land. The sea will be my vacation as the world of water is to you."

"How will you vacation?" he asked.

"I like to go fishing but until now have not had much time to enjoy the call of the sea," she observed while she turned to look out the windows as a tumult of birds pursued minnows along the shore.

"The call should be answered," he agreed.

"You have helped me to listen," she added. "Maybe someday I'll see you on the beach."

"I can't resist the call," he observed. "By answering, you have made the right decision. You have altered the course my ship of life is taking. Now we are both focusing on fishing. The cook at the work site for building my lane and cabin would like fresh catches. I also like to catch and cook fish. Our new lives begin."

Flashing a smile Jake would remember, she walked to a counter, picked up the grouper sandwich and brought it to his table before getting distracted by other customers.

After the meal, Jake returned to his room at the resort. He felt another door had opened and he had entered a different view of life from which there was no return.

He phoned Will, finding him finishing work for the night. "All preparations are in order," he explained. "Everything will take place at once—both the lane construction and cabin building. We could meet you at the site tomorrow."

"Great news," exclaimed Jake. "See you there."

Following the rest of the night when there was little sleep but much anticipation, Jake gave up the effort for rest and at the very first sign of light brightening the outside world he started preparing breakfast in the room. He perked coffee, boiled porridge and added some toast topped with jam and homey. Without dreaming or planning over a cup of coffee, he took some with him to savor while driving to the wilderness area he had purchased for no cost. *Calley said the land was paid for years earlier*, he recalled. *Good works often—maybe always—last forever and take turns or blossom in ways unforeseen.*

As Jake expected, there was already established a well-marked path providing a route to follow on the land close to shore. *This access trail will outline the lane*, he noted. *There's no need to mark the route any more than can already be seen.*

Will's crew starts early, thought Jake, as the sounds of boat's motors and voices grew louder. He stepped out into the open and was greeted by a work crew in action. Some boats were pulled up on shore while others were arriving.

Deciding to stay out of the way unless his help was called for, he sat on high sandy ground and watched while first the supplies and equipment he had purchased were placed nearby. Also, a small boat with outboard motor was pulled up on shore before being covered by a tarp. Supplies also were covered.

Farther along the beach, a main camp started to be established with tents being set up. In the midst of the action Will Jenkins approached Jake.

"Life is exciting," stated the gruff yet exuberant foreman as he greeted Jake.

"You certainly don't waste time," replied Jake, before Will also sat.

"Life is short," said Will. "We should make the best of it."

"And you have," said Jake. "How do you stay in a good mood?"

"Work," he answered. "I enjoy building—making things. I'm uncomfortable at parties. I don't like talking to have fun. I like doing something. Talking, to me is the same as using any other tool, such as a screwdriver or hammer. I use these things for a purpose. I enjoy working with a hammer but I don't use it idly. I make something. I consider words the same way. They're interesting if they have a purpose but I can't see sitting around doing nothing but carrying on idle conversation. That's like tossing a hammer up into the air, and catching it over and over again. You seem to be much the same."

"I agree with you," said Jake, "although sometimes I'll use talk for an exchange of opinions—or company."

"Hadn't thought o' that," mused Will. "Maybe when I retire I'll consider such an idea but I don't plan to retire."

"You said before," noted Jake, "work keeps you in a good mood. There's always trouble. Some people stay there and let it get them down. I have made a choice to live above the fray—the dilemmas, maybe as a boat sailing above rough water and, if you can't always see the lighthouse ahead, you have to have faith that it's there."

"I guess that's what I do too," said Will. "Fortunately not all water is rough.

Today the sea is beautiful and we are preparing for a great new project."

Standing, Will said, "I've been here before when others have tried to buy this land. There is a trail next to the water. Does that mark the lane we are to put in?"

"Yes," answered Jake. "When Roger Tomkins recommends people, I must always listen to him."

"Maybe you could show me now where you want your cabin and the full design of it?" suggested Will.

"That's easy to do," replied Jake, before he stood. He walked with Will to a central foundation Jake had previously located. Will put in stakes, as Jake talked. "We could use the old foundation as much as possible," he said. "Apparently there was a line of cabins. We are only building one—the first in the line. That must've been where the family lived. A side door on the east would enter into a kitchen with a low counter facing the one main room. Screened windows would be all along the front, facing west toward the Gulf. On the northeast corner, there are to be a propane fireplace and wood stove backed by the washroom with a door and window. Windows are on all sides. Two bedrooms would be at the back, or east, with air conditioner in between and steps going up to a third bedroom above the first two."

Will, who had been sketching while Jake spoke, asked, "Is this an accurate outline of the cabin you just described?'

"Perfect," he exclaimed. "We both see the same structure."

"We had a small boat and motor not being used much," added Will. "If you could use it, we have given it to you.

We've pulled it up on sand, added a full gas tank and covered both with a tarp."

"Thank you," replied Jake. "A boat will add new possibilities for fishing."

"Our cook, George Sloan, wants to receive any extra fish you catch. Don't bother to fillet them. For him, that's just another part of food preparation. He can supply you with roast pork. He's good at adding wild boar to the roasted food supply."

"With pork and fish, the meals will be great here," observed Jake.

"There are always grits and baked beans," added Will. "They're basic with any meal."

"We're going to have a great time," exclaimed Jake.

"We get paid to do this," noted Will, "but not one of us considers it work.

This is our life and we enjoy it. At night you might hear some guitar strumming and singing. These culprits don't look pretty but some of them sing that way."

"I'm going to regret having your construction finished," concluded Jake.

"Every day brings its own work and holiday," noted Will. "We can't always tell the difference. I know for certain, however, the time has come for me to get this project under way. I'll keep checking with you for your opinions." He turned and started walking toward the camp being constructed.

I have a camp to set up also, recalled Jake. He walked to the supplies the crew had brought in by boat. The first tent he put up was to be his shelter until the cabin was completed. The second tent was to store equipment and other supplies.

Connections from the main camp brought in fresh water along with electricity. He also had to assemble the propane stove. Half of his tent would be for cooking.

Jake slept poorly the first two nights, until his camp started to roughly resemble a residence, as it should be, until the cabin was completed and he could be established in his permanent dwelling. Meals would come out of cans and be heated on the stove. Coffee kept the morning in order and evening was greeted with a glass of beer to sooth tired muscles while he took time, brief as it was, to notice the beauty the setting sun added to a landscape filled with more splendor than could be noted completely during any occasion.

Much of my main tent is filled by a kitchen space with a washing area, he observed. *There's a fridge and stove. Taps are on lines bringing in fresh water from the central camp. Other connections add electricity from the work site's generators. The rest of my tent will be a living quarters, having a sleeping bag on an air mattress in addition to comfortable chairs, a table and lamp.*

With the front of each tent open I can see the Gulf, he noted with satisfaction. He sat to rest after adding final adjustments to his temporary yet quite comfortable residence. *I should soon sign out of my room at the resort,* he resolved. *I can walk to my car, following the strip of sand that actually winds endlessly beside the sea. Of course, I can also follow the lane where the crew is working.*

I have an opportunity here to go fishing. This area is my home. So many other people have felt the same way. Happy at their home and it is here. The Timucuans are the first remembered. Their remnant people, along with the Calusas and others, joined Creeks coming south from places like present day Alabama. They became known as Seminoles. Families through all these generations, kept the memories and records. Of particular interest to me of course is the Stonebear family. They were friends with my ancestors, the Sands. All these people call this place home. On a past foundation I'm building a cabin. This is where I'll stay. I've been called, like so many others, by the sea. I can't resist the call yet I'm distracted. I keep feeling I'm late for something. I have not completed my journey to get here. I'm late for what I'm called to do. Why should I be concerned? Someday I'll be as all the others who considered this area to be home and are not here now. Nothing has been left behind to mark their passing by this way except in some cases mounds of shells. What does it matter if a person living here in the past, dining on oysters, throwing the emptied shells on a pile, did not finish all he or she had to do before completing their purpose for life at this home? On this earth clearly these lifetimes don't matter because nothing, or very little, apparently is here. But this is not the place where life's journey takes place. The only schedule that matters is spiritual and it is our purpose to keep improving, learning and in our own way become better than before. The connecting spirit to all unique people and parts is the Creator and the only life that matters is spiritual. We neglect this truth at our own peril. Only spiritual life and world last forever. A person's struggles on earth might leave behind only a pile of shells but each life is unique and is connected in addition to being recorded.

Looking around at his tent camp having a view to the sea with its constant invitation, Jake stood and realized, *I'm not ready to settle down and go fishing. I've left something behind on my journey. Time has come for me to go for a walk.*

Answering the call, he walked down to the sea. He turned westward. Proceeding at a fast pace, feeling he was late for something, he proceeded forward, joining all other parts. They were also moving. Waves surged toward shore and crested before crashing onto sand, sending flows forward before they turned back to be replaced by the next onrush of water. Sandpipers chased the flows in a search for food, particularly coquinas. A salty breeze moved from the sea and rustled palm leaves along with other foliage.

Jake kept walking, moving as were all surrounding parts. He was just one moving with the others and joined them. Gulls screamed and dove for minnows splashing at the surface to avoid fish attacking below. Pelicans soared above waves. Occasionally the hunters would dive for a fish. Sometimes a gull would land on a pelican's head and try to steal part of the catch.

Jake walked until he proceeded beyond some restaurants and resorts. He reached the place where he had rented a room. He sat on a sand bank and watched the restless sea. *Like the water*, he thought, *I don't rest and have that feeling of being late for an important part of my life even when there is no immediate evidence of any reason for rushing. I'm seeking all the time. This search, however, has left me only tired.*

Shadows of evening were gathering and lengthened while Jake walked back to the tent camp. Both sky and water caught crimson hues from the sun as it moved toward the horizon. All colors deepened until they became lost amid night's murkiness.

Following a night when sleep was elusive, Jake welcomed morning. He made breakfast with its highlight being coffee. *I have too much to accomplish for sleep to find me*, he concluded while he watched the rising sun dispel shadows and bring warmth to a new day.

When all structures of his own camp were in place, he walked over to the main area and its kitchen where the cook, George Sloan was testing some propane stoves. In front of this covered area, there was a fire pit topped by a skewer for roasting.

At Jake's approach, George looked at him then upward, as if perceiving wisdom from a realm unknown by other, lesser people and joked, "I'm all-seeing and all-knowing and I perceive your name to be Jake Sands."

"A far-seeing cook is the best mystic leader to have in a camp," replied Jake, "and I perceive you to be George Sloan."

"You're one too," laughed the jovial man, who always seemed to have a smile on his whiskered face and spark in his dark eyes. His hair was black and as tangled as his beard.

"I have beer to share if you guys are short now or at any time," offered Jake.

"Thank you," said George. "We are amply supplied in that and most ways and you can help yourself any time but we only enjoy such refreshments as beer in the evenings after the day's work has been done so you don't get a crooked cabin to live in."

"Thanks for the offer," said Jake. "I see evening approaching, eventually, and I didn't want to keep enjoying such a luxury as a refreshing beer for the evening unless you had some available also."

"We're going to get along well," proclaimed George. "We share what we have be it a little or a lot."

"I'd better get back," said Jake. "I took a can out of the cooler and wouldn't want such a refreshment to spoil."

"Waste not," stated George, as Jake turned and started walking back to his newly assembled residence.

Jake picked up the can he had removed from the cooler. He was pleased to discover the drink continued to be cold. He selected what would likely be his favorite chair as it was placed in shade from palms and provided a full view of the Gulf.

A new world has opened, he mused after sitting and opening the can. He sipped it slowly, while watching backs of dolphins occasionally break through the surface, to obtain air before submerging again under small waves moving toward shore. Almost always, there was background music of waves splashing along sand. Pelicans flew past while clouds moved overhead, picking up colors from the evening sun. Shades of red deepened while spreading across sky and sea. These hues were gathered back by the setting sun. Night erased most colors and light.

Jake opened a second can of beer, letting it bring him closer to sleep and maybe the first full night of sleep in his almost completed tent camp. *Amazing to think,* he recalled, *that dolphins and others, such as whales, were in earlier times land animals and related to hippos. Dolphins are sleek and swim majestically yet these animals have to surface in order to breathe just like people, particularly those seafarers who answer the call to the sea and are particularly happy when they are on a boat.*

Enjoying the breeze continuing to rattle palm leaves and bring freshness to the night, Jake resolved, *I'll go to stores tomorrow to get extra supplies and I want to start a garden. I'd like to get prepared to make Roger Tomkins' celebration sandwich. To get started, I'll follow his methods. For pickles, I'll grow cucumbers in addition to onions and peppers and I'll have to buy dill, garlic, vinegar and salt. For chili sauce, along with onions and peppers, I'll of course have to grow tomatoes and buy celery, salt, cinnamon, brown sugar and vinegar. To make sandwiches I'll start out by buying the bread.*

Maybe tonight for the first time, he hoped, *I can actually get some sleep but there's just so much to do catching sleep is a difficult pursuit. I'll keep renting the room at the resort for a while to get started. I'll heat some beans then have a meal of beans and toast before concluding another wonderful day. I'll try to enjoy each one to the fullest. Although there's much to do, I want to put in the garden.*

The first rays of sunlight next morning found Jake finishing a breakfast of porridge and toast. He cleaned up his tent then started walking along the trail to get his car. He drove to nurseries and garden centers where he bought necessary supplies to plant his garden and also extra items for making a celebration sandwich while his garden produced the next ingredients along with many other meals.

Pleased with his completed work, he went to the same restaurant for a noontime meal. The sunlight of his new adventure took on a gray shade when he noticed Tess had done what she planned and stopped working there. He again ordered grouper sandwich with cheese and watched the Gulf bring waves to shore without apparent change, although Jake felt he had lost something in not seeing the person he had been hoping to meet again.

He drove back to the start of the trail leading to his camp and was pleased to see members of the crew working on the lane. Back at his tents, he threw himself into preparing a garden. Gradually the tonic of hard work allowed the sun's rays to dispel the gray mood he had caught at the restaurant.

After borrowing a wheel barrel from the crew along with using his own new tools, he hauled muck from borders of the inlet and filled an area where he would put in plants and seed. *In addition to muck*, he resolved, *for fertilizer I'll use ashes from my fire pit and also bury any extra fish parts from filleting.*

After seeds had been placed in muck along with tomato plants, the cook arrived to check this new source of fresh vegetables. "If I'm going to be in one place long, I always plant a garden because there is no substitute for fresh food," noted George, after both men sat on a palm log to observe Jake's planting work. "I've never had success growing tomatoes."

"The secret with them is to plant them deep, burying about a third or one half the stem in the ground," suggested Jake. "The covered part of the stem sends out roots and secures strength. I've also planted onions, peppers and cucumbers. This is now your garden. You can use it to help provide fresh vegetables."

"Very considerate of you," exclaimed George. "I can supply you with fresh, wild hog."

"That's a treat I'm looking forward to," replied Jake. "We'll share what we have and end with some tasty food."

"That's my job of course," noted George, "but as the other crew members on this team, we enjoy the work we do. During one of my first wilderness trips, we discovered, when we were out in wild country, no one knew how to prepare food or even make coffee. That's when I decided to never let that situation happen again and I learned to cook."

"Using the garden, I plan to make pickles and Chili sauce," observed Jake. "I met a fellow called Roger Tomkins and he told me the recipes."

"Hopefully soon, I can say I met a fellow called Jake Sands and he told me about these recipes," added George, with a large smile showing under his whiskers.

"For a batch of the world's greatest chili sauce," explained Jake, "you mix together about twelve cut up tomatoes, one red pepper, one stalk of celery and six onions then add them to a pot with two cups cider vinegar, one tablespoon of salt, two tablespoons of cinnamon, and two cups brown sugar before boiling the mixture until its thick and put it into sterile jars."

"And the pickles?" asked George.

"For a batch of pickles," explained Jake, "you start with about four pounds of small cucumbers. Wash them as everything else and cut a little off each end. Keep them cold overnight to add crispness. The next day, place them in hot sterilized jars, with two cloves of garlic at the bottom along with dill seed and a few peppercorns. Add to the jars a slice or two of red pepper and sweet onion in addition to sprays of dill. Next fill the jars with a boiling mixture of four cups white vinegar, eight cups water and almost a cup of coarse pickling salt. Store the jars a few weeks to get full flavor. I can write out these recipes for you."

"I can remember them and thank you for sharing your ideas," replied George. "I'll buy some chili sauce and pickles to get started"

"I've had to do that also," added Jake. "If you want to come to the tent, I'll make you a special sandwich. For the preparation, if you have some, you could bring some of your famous roasted, wild hog."

"Coming right up," shouted George, before he left. Jake walked to his tent. In a short time George arrived with his contribution.

Later, the two men sat in the shade provided by palms. Each man enjoyed a celebration sandwich accompanied by beer. "These are a celebration," exclaimed George, "and the members of the crew are going to get them. You have added a great addition to my cooking. Thank you for sharing this discovery. Sandwiches go well with beer," he added, before he emptied his glass. "I'm going back now to prepare a celebration for the crew. Thanks, Jake."

"Don't forget you now have a garden for fresh vegetables," noted Jake.

"Your tent is a wonderful place to visit," shouted George, before he hastened back to his camp.

Jake put on a swimsuit and walked to the beach. He dove into the waves where he always felt welcomed. Resurfacing after swimming through greenish hued water touched with amber tones from sunlight, he thought, *every time I come to the sea, I wonder why I'm away so long. Maybe I'm a seafarer like so many others who feel called by the sea and are fully at home nowhere else, particularly on land away from even the sight of ocean.*

Returning to shore, he enjoyed walking on the sand formed from broken shells that became warm but not as hot as bits of stone comprising sand in so many other places. *Even sharks teeth form part of the beach here*, noted Jake as he used the towel to get dry. *Amazing to consider the story a piece of land holds not just in human accounts but with the environment also. So many people think distance means travel yet there are often, usually, as many stories to be found when a person traces the journey of any small area of land or sea. I can sit up at my tent camp and consider the many people who have lived here and in their own time looked out upon the ocean as I do and wonder about those who came before them. Will has given me a statement for the cost of this project when it is finished. Tomorrow, I'll go out and get the payment.*

From the shade of palms, Jake watched the surrounding world as time moved and with it so did color. Hues of red deepened and became brighter until this shade filled both sky and water as the sun moved into purple haze along the horizon. Waves lessened until the ocean became as calm as it ever appeared for a realm that never rested. *Water is always moving*, noted Jake, before he picked up his cast net. *Time to catch some bait*.

He walked to the water's edge where he was joined by a great blue heron and a snowy egret. "Three fishermen should be able to catch something," said Jake to his companions before he threw out the first cast. It brought in more than he could have hoped for particularly with a first throw. In the net were scaled sardines or greenbacks and some mullet. Jake fed the minnows to the egret and mullet to the heron until both birds became full and flew back to rest for the night. Jake saved some green backs and mullet for bait.

Getting his fishing pole, he put it in the boat before pulling it to the water's edge. He stepped inside, sat down with fishing equipment and bait then started rowing. In deep water, he dropped a mullet on a hook and let out line while he rowed back to shore.

Sitting on the sand, he watched the area of color where the sun had vanished taking most bright colors away at the same time. Remnant hues faded into night's arrival. Soon light started to return as color appeared along the eastern horizon where the moon started to rise. Almost matching the sun in brightness, this orb lost colors while ascending the sky.

Caught almost unprepared, Jake suddenly noticed the line had tightened and pole was bending. He pulled the pole back to set the hook and something large and strong pulled back. A battle started that soon brought George and two other members of the crew.

"Mysterious sea," mused George. "We never know what's out there and some of it thinks we are on the menu."

"Probably what we've hooked now thinks we are part of the food supply as we think of them because this is likely a shark," offered Jake.

"Grilled shark stakes—and fresh too," shouted one of the crew. "George, you're a great cook."

"I get a lot of help from Jake," he admitted.

"Help or not, the food on this trip is even better than usual," exclaimed the worker.

"Do you think the crew would want steaks tonight?" asked George.

"They always seem to be hungry," answered the other man. "Particularly, with food as this."

"Steaks it'll be then," decided George. "We just need the steaks to be not quite as fresh as they are now."

"It's turning," observed Jake. It's coming to shore. Let's make sure we dine on it and not the other way about."

"I'll get a rope," stated one man, before he ran back to camp. In a short time, he returned carrying a long hauling line.

A wall of water shot from the dark sea as the powerful fish lashed out at the approaching border of sand. Pulling on the line, Jake got the creature's head turned and pointed to the sand where a rope was sent out, catching around gills and helping to haul the sleek, dark form from the water.

"We could take it right up to camp," said George. "Want steaks tonight Jake," he asked.

"I would like to try your steaks but not tonight, thank you," he replied.

"Good catch, Jake," said George. "You'll have to go fishing more often.

"I will," he replied. "Right now, I think I hear a boat ride calling."

While the other men hauled the new food supply up to camp, Jake stepped into his boat, pointed the bow toward open sea then stared the motor. He began what for him was something he would always do, and all people practice in different ways. He left the place where cares and worries dwelt and traveled away to view his life according to what he would do if he was completely free.

With bow pointed toward the place where there was nothing but a line marking the horizon, he at first drove at slow speed but gradually opened the motor to full blast. Against the bow there was a slight tap as last remnants of swells from storms long forgotten splashed while being sliced by the impact of the boat. Above, there was a full moon in a starlit sky. This panorama of light was mirrored on the almost calm water, turning the vessel's progress to one of a dreamlike journey upon a silver sea. *I must do this more often*, thought Jake, as he left all cares and plans behind and just joined the wonder of his surroundings. The speed of the boat sent a slight rush of air against Jake's face, while he became as much as he could be part of the sky above and sky mirrored below. *I have been given a great opportunity*, he mused. *There is a chance to have a home here in the place where the environment provides the best for our lives. I can't just enjoy the opportunities. I must work with them and build something as great as what I have been given. At least I'll try. I'll try to protect the greatness of the environment and leave it better than I found it. I'll work to make this area a better place. That's my objective.*

A person's achievements might not be seen at the time or era when they occur yet they would be stored on the spiritual side as I've learned by getting lost in the wilderness that life is not really physical, it's spiritual. All the people who lived here before me might have been missed by those coming later had there not been left behind great mounds of shells. The accomplishments of these people are listed and last on the spiritual side where all these lives are recorded and continue. Each person's role is to do the best possible under circumstances and work for improvement while staying on course with the Creator and not turning away. This presence is certainly visible tonight. I wish I could see as clearly during the storms and other troubles. Tomorrow I'll pay Will for his contributions although he and his crew have given much more with their company than items listed on a bill.

Out a long way on the silver sea, Jake stopped, turned the boat and looked for a sign of his location. *I should be more careful during future trips*, he reasoned. *Fortunately I caught a shark and it is being roasted. I can see the light coming from George's cooking fire. There are also other electric lights from their camp. I must return. I have much to do and I almost feel as if I'm just beginning and maybe late for much of my life.*

Not wanting to miss such a majestic night when the environment seemed to be completely at rest, Jake slept in a chair outside his tent refreshed by a salty breeze moving to shore from the Gulf. He awoke to see the red and yellow hues of sunrise.

After breakfast, he followed the marked lane and walked back to his car. Work had begun to provide vehicle access to his cabin. He drove to his room at the resort where he enjoyed a shower before paying for and closing his booking.

Leaving again, he visited a bank. He withdrew payment to give to Will and the crew for the building of his cabin along with access to it. At other places he purchased more supplies including extra ice for coolers and a bucket of live shrimp for bait. *The days are here for fishing*, he concluded, having checked off required purchases on his list.

Before returning to camp, he decided to stop at an oyster bar for a meal. *Since Tess, or really Tessa Taber, isn't at the usual restaurant, I'll try a different place*, he reasoned, before opening the door to the bar. Inside he was struck by the commotion. Noise was constant. Stale air was filled with scents of cooked food and alcohol. *I do not belong inside places anymore*, Jake realized. *This is all suddenly foreign and abrasive.*

Florida

Seeing people leaving a table, Jake sat where they had been. Discomfort of an unwashed area was soon swept away by a woman who removed the used dishes then ran a cloth across the table. She seemed to be average in all ways except in her adaptation to a life of constant work, whereby she could be constantly active without appearing to tire. Her hair and eyes were light brown; she was of medium height and weight.

"I'm Martha," she explained. "I'm also your server."

After placing in front of him a clean knife and fork along with glass of water followed by a menu, she asked, "Anything from the bar?"

"Draft, please," he answered, "then the special of oyster chowder, snapper dinner and key-lime pie."

"Good choices," she exclaimed, without making notes. "Those are the best in the house—best anywhere."

"All good news," he replied. "I'm Jake Sands. Pleased to meet you."

I did not realize how much I've changed, mused Jake after the draft arrived and he sipped the cold drink, welcoming something familiar in a foreign place. *I don't belong here anymore—if I ever did. I now must be outside to be at peace. I see and feel no peace here; yet, for others, this situation is what they look forward to as best entertainment with noise, shouting and action. Immediately, I miss the silence of the world where I now live with the welcome additions of a cardinal's song and the sound of waves splashing along the shore.*

"Special is arriving," proclaimed Martha before she placed aromatic foods on the table in front of Jake.

"Thank you," he said. "Everything looks wonderful."

"Because we are busy, I'm leaving the bill also and you pay on the way out."

"OK," he replied, before she hastened away.

The food was delicious and he dined contentedly although the surrounding noise constantly assaulted his attempt to ignore it. After finishing the meal, leaving a large tip and paying the bill, he realized he was rushing to the exit. Outside, the cool, seemingly clean air greeted him and welcomed him back to the world where he found his new life.

He returned to his tent where he felt it welcomed him with a feeling he had been away too long. He slept soundly and the next day he walked to the main camp and asked Will to come over for a visit when he had time.

The day had progressed toward evening when the large man approached Jake's camp. "George has sent you a thank you note," said Will, before the two men sat on chairs outside the tents. Keeping one, Will gave Jake a paper plate topped by a large sandwich. "George said you told him about these special, celebration sandwiches and they are special. He has been making them for the crew and they have become a favorite item."

"Thank you both," replied Jake, after giving the foreman a can of beer then opening a second can. After tasting the sandwich, Jake said, "There are cooks who prepare food. Then there are people, such as George, who make meals a special part of a day because cooking is not a function to make a meal but a sharing of some great accomplishments in life. That guy doesn't cook to live, he lives to cook and this sandwich really is a celebration of the joy he finds in preparing food."

"Wow," exclaimed Will. "He can prepare it and you are just as talented at describing it. We work hard and we do appreciate good food. We also thank you for bringing us shark steaks. There's nothing better than fresh food. If the other batch was any fresher, it might have tried dining on us. We will appreciate more sharks or any fish you catch."

"Knowing people want the food gives a special joy to fishing," replied Jake. "I'll try to catch all the sea wants to share. Speaking of sharing, I have a thank you note to give you."

Jake gave the foreman the payment, and the large man first put it into his pocket then said, "Payment is early but thank you. Usually this occurs after the work is completed."

"I usually try to do everything early," said Jake, before he supplied another can of beer.

"Everything about this job has been the best possible," noted Will. "I suspect the men will be sorry to leave."

"I've enjoyed your company," observed Jake, "and George does make a great sandwich."

"He said he had to buy all the ingredients but will always try when available to get vegetables out of the garden," added Will. "Thanks for the payment. Maybe I'll get back to camp. I'll report to George you approve of his creations."

"He can send you both over any time," said Jake, as the man was leaving.

The cabin is being formed, noted Jake. *I actually enjoy this tent camp but residence at the cabin will be an entirely new phase of my life. It's an adventure of my life, built upon works of others I fully acknowledge and from such a great past I wildly anticipate the excitement of my life. It's not separate but it's something unique only I can build. As each person, I must walk my own trail. I enjoy my journey and would not, could not, trade with anyone.*

We would each pick our own troubles and likely we did if, as I think happens, people design what they want to do before they leave the spiritual side and come to earth with the purpose of developing areas that could be improved.

The moon was rising. The orb seemed to lift itself out of shades of red to become a light, sending a silver trail to the tent camp. *I'm in far too good a mood to sleep*, observed Jake. *The sea is calling me and I'll answer the call. I have frozen mullet saved for the heron. I can use some for bait and the time has come to go fishing.*

After loading his equipment and stepping into his boat, he rowed far out onto the silver sea and dropped in the baited line. Returning to shore, he pulled the craft back to the place it was stored. He added a chair to his equipment and returned to the water's edge where he sat then tightened the line leading to the silver trail on its way to the moon as it kept climbing into the night sky.

This is as beautiful as it is peaceful, mused Jake while he held the pole and watched the water. The line tightened and started to go out from the reel when George arrived. He also carried a chair.

"Saw you out in the boat," said the cook, in greeting. "Pleased to hear you enjoy my celebration sandwiches."

"I'm pleased, too, you sent one over with Will," replied Jake. "Your cooking is a celebration and you help also with the fishing. I think you have some shark steaks pulling on this line."

"Fresh is good," said George. "I don't want them to be overly fresh, however. Food is something I prepare to be eaten and I don't want it to try and eat me."

"A shark is one of the few fish that would try to dine on the cook," added Jake. "Of course, if pork was too fresh, it would try to dine on the cook, too."

"Yes," agreed George. "Food can be dangerous and I always try to be the cook and not the cooked."

"Shark steaks are fresh and impatient," noted Jake, when his pole bent and thrashed wildly.

"The sea never rests," stated George, "and you are faster at picking up fish than the guy at the meat counter in any store."

Florida

"Service is faster here and fish are fresher," said Jake. "Do you want to feel the freshness?" he asked, giving George the pole.

"That thing is big," George exclaimed, putting his full strength into not being pulled out to sea.

"Stay with it as long as you enjoy it," said Jake. "I'm going to sleep for the night."

"What?" George shouted. "You're not leaving me here?"

"Actually I'm just going to get a rope," Jake said.

"You going to lasso this thing?" inquired George.

"Just the tail," replied Jake. "If we catch it, we can pull it by the tail up to your cook tent, as we did before."

Jake walked away yet returned quickly carrying a strong rope. "Is the shark coming toward shore?" he asked.

"Sometimes quickly," the cook answered. "Then he goes out again. We are both tiring. He's coming in."

A splash close to shore confirmed George's opinion. He reeled in line rapidly just before a second splash brought the two men into action.

"I'll try to bring it in," said the cook. He hauled on the pole just as the fish turned, bringing the creature's head up on the sand. He kept the line taut, giving Jake a chance to drop a loop of rope around the tail. Both men pulled on the rope and started dragging the large fish to the cook's tent.

"I'll leave both pole and shark with you," said Jake. "I won't risk any unhooking until later."

"Thanks for your delivery of fresh steaks," shouted George.

"Thanks for shopping at Sands Lodge," replied Jake, before he walked back to his tent.

Jake washed, rested and was soon sleeping soundly. In first light of dawn, he enjoyed breakfast of baked beans and fried potatoes.

Sitting on a chair in front of his tent, he sipped coffee in content while he watched the land and water respond to the rising sun's warming rays. Dolphins returned to break through the surface to get air while crossing in front of the building site. Pelicans patrolled as usual and above all action below, a frigate bird soared.

Rather than being busy all the time, reasoned Jake, *I want to enjoy more time similar to today when I just join in the pulse of the land and sea, connect with them and rest in the peace of the wilderness. The splash of waves upon the sand is the most soothing of sounds and I can feel as unhurried as the wisp of clouds drifting across the seemingly endless blue sky.*

"They said at the main camp that you are Jake Sands," said a woman's voice, catching Jake in a rare moment when he was joining the calm of his surroundings.

"They told you correctly," answered Jake, as he turned around and was struck by beauty different from that of wilderness but just as mysterious. She had black hair pulled back and tied away from her face by a red cap. Highlighting seemingly perfect features, her black eyes flashed, when she said, "I wanted to meet the wild man I saw twice before along the trail but tried to avoid. I would have continued avoiding you but Roger Tomkins, where I park my car, said you are wild but not dangerous."

"He's right on both counts," confirmed Jake, before he got her a chair then brought them both a can of beer.

"Service is good at the Sands Lodge," she said, with a smile that trapped him. "Roger told me your amazing story. He knew I would be interested because, as he, I also tried but failed to buy this land. It's one of my favorite places. I got to know Roger because he lets me park my car at his place. Previously, I had told him about a wild man I had seen and stayed away from, along the trail."

"Generally, us wild creatures are not dangerous," affirmed Jake. "Wild bears stay away from and don't bother people. When people feed bears, they start to see people as a source of food, such animals are considered spoiled bears and are no longer wild. They might harm people."

"From what Roger told me I wanted to meet you," repeated the woman. "As I have mentioned, he said you were wild but not dangerous—I suppose the same as the bears. I'm Cynthia, actually Cindy Terrance."

"Pleased to actually meet you," replied Jake. "I tried to talk to you when we saw each other the first time but you were unapproachable."

"You do make a lasting first impression," she exclaimed, laughing. "You looked to be as wild as the wilderness."

"I'm pleased you returned," he said. "I'm building a cabin here on the foundation of the previous Sands Lodge."

"Yes," she noted. "Roger, as I said, told me your amazing story."

"I'll have to thank Roger for his good messages," he replied. "Part of my amazing story is to have you here. More beer?"

"Actually, I came prepared," she replied. "After Roger told me I should meet you, I went back to the store and brought supplies for margaritas. Do you like them?"

"Oh, I'm sure I will—today," he said. "While you make preparations, I'm going to make sandwiches."

"Oh thank you," she said before opening her backpack.

Cindy worked outside, helped by a table Jake brought for her then he went into his tent to quickly put together the specialty Roger had shown him.

Retuning with two paper plates each topped by a large sandwich, he gave one to his surprised guest, before he sat again.

"Wow," she exclaimed. "Everything about you is wild, just the same as this out-of-the-wilderness sandwich."

"Roger Tomkins showed me how to make this treat," he explained. "We call it our celebration sandwich."

"Rightly named—for sure," she exclaimed before giving him a glass of margarita.

"Thank you," he said. "Service is good here at the Sands Lodge."

After sampling the sandwich, she said, "Taste's as great as it looks."

He sipped the drink and added, "Same is true with your wonderful margarita."

"A celebration day, Jake," exclaimed Cindy, holding up her glass to salute the Gulf. "What a great place—and today I met the wild man I ran away from the first time."

"I'll have to thank Roger for the good things he must be saying about me," repeated Jake.

"He was saying good things and I'm thinking them," she said, smiling again in a way that matched her beauty to the surrounding land, water and sky. All parts of the environment seemed to be in a mood of celebrating life, blending together in harmony.

The sun continued its journey across the sky, dolphins swam again past the site, pelicans soared and eventually colors of evening gathered to join the sun as it slowly sank beyond a red haze along the horizon.

After enjoying margaritas while sitting on the chairs and becoming part of the changing landscape, Jake and his visitor moved into the tent where a new celebration started. For Jake, in the morning, he thought he had reached a special plateau of happiness while he prepared and served breakfast.

Florida

Cindy prepared her backpack for returning to the trail. Before leaving, she and Jake enjoyed a first cup of coffee while sitting on chairs in front of the tent. First bright colors of morning gradually became more muted as the sun started its climb into what seemed to have become one perfect day after another.

Jake was thinking he and Cindy made a great catch, had both hooked each other and were about to start reeling home when Cindy cut both lines. Casually she said, "I suppose I don't act much like a woman who is getting married next month."

The sunlit day clouded for Jake before he said, "Should this have been mentioned yesterday?"

"There's something about this place that is special," she replied. "I felt at home here. I was free to be myself. When I saw the wild man on the trail I, maybe as anyone, wanted to meet you but had to have some security first. That I got from Roger Tomkins."

"I thought I had caught a keeper until you threw the hook just now," said Jake, after refilling their cups.

"I came here—and all other things fell away, leaving me with my life and what it would be to have no ties at least for a short time," she explained. "I have no regrets."

"I regret loosing such a beautiful possibility, great fish," added Jake.

"I'm some kind of a fish now?" she asked, laughing.

"Recently more than before, I've come to see life as a fishing trip," explained Jake. "The easiest part of life is to just be alive and that's what many people do. They apply no more effort than required for each day's meal. Each person sets his or her own course. Very few fishermen or fisherwomen catch most fish and this is the way of life. Few people see the full extent of possibilities because not many individuals set sails for such courses. With you, I saw a great fish or an unusually good possibility."

"As I was saying before," observed Cindy, "I got to see who I would be if I were free—divorced probably."

"You wouldn't be on the market any longer than you wanted to be," stated Jake. "I'd cast a line in your direction."

"Well, wild man," she exclaimed, "I'll wear that compliment with as much pride as any ring. Others can't see it but I'll know it's there."

"I'll remember your spirit but also the beauty that wraps it—the packaging," he added.

After sipping more of the drink, Cindy looked at the sea without seeing it because her thoughts were back at the other end of the trail in her usual life. "I should explain the word marriage," she said. "I'm rally marrying my husband. We've been living together for about three years. That ties us by common law. My partner owns and runs an art business. He does oil paintings and I prefer watercolors."

"Your interest in beauty brings you to the wilderness," noted Jake.

"That summarizes the life I left behind for this holiday," she added. Standing, she said, "I should start walking or there will be a search party. We all have our own trail to follow."

"You're going to swim away?" he asked, smiling.

"Enough of the fish, Jake," she said, flashing a smile to blend in with the surrounding landscape.

Cindy had just left when Will arrived. He too received coffee and both men sat down to watch the sun mark time of day by stages in a journey across the sky. Smiling and staring at Jake, Will said, "The men of the crew and I want to book a room at the sands lodge. It's a special place—casts a spell. Beautiful women are caught by it and they spend the night— unfortunately with Jake this time; but aside from that, we've all been in a good mood here. You once told me your home was not the cabin but the wilderness surrounding it—and such is the lure—the tonic of this place. Each one catches some depth of this special area—the wilderness. Only wilderness is pure enough to have such power over people."

"You're a builder," said Jake. "You're also a poet."

"Jake Sands," exclaimed Will. "I and the men are pleased to have met you because you are the first person we know who has his home outside of his house."

Laughing, Jake exclaimed, "You understand. My home is the wilderness. The cabin keeps the rain off. Our truest home is wilderness and we don't see it for what it is. We cut, or allow it to be cut to get logs. We also scoop it away as overburden in a search for oil or other mining pursuits."

"If I and the crew learned as much from each person with whom we worked we would probably get too conceited to work together any more," joked Will.

"Could I make you a sandwich?" asked Jake.

"I certainly hope so," he replied.

Jake hastened into his tent, returned with two cans of beer, gave one to the foreman, placed the other by his own chair then rushed back to the tent. In a surprisingly short time, he returned, carrying two paper plates topped by sandwiches.

"You know how to live in the wilderness, Jake," exclaimed Will as he received a sandwich then Jake also sat and the two men enjoyed a large snack.

"People say, I'm a man who works all the time and doesn't like parties or holidays," said Will. "After being here at Sands Lodge, I realize that such a description of me is completely accurate and I wouldn't have life any other way. If I went to a party or holiday, I couldn't possibly have any more fun than I've had here at the Sands Lodge—Resort—whatever it's called. I actually have more fun than people on holidays because they often do nothing but sit around and talk. I have lots of exciting activities to pursue and learn something at the same time, finding life to be a sailing trip around the world."

"Your understanding of events exceeds that of most people," observed Jake.

"Your wisdom lies in your awareness that your home is outside your house," said Will, before he finished the drink. Jake hastily brought them each another.

"I should add," said Will, "by the way, thank you for the beer—and sandwich; but, as I was saying, I'm not knocking the art of doing nothing. I often do it. However when I pursue that event I do it on purpose so it is an activity such as a pursuit of taking time to enjoy our surroundings, or think, along with relaxing and resting. These occasions are not just a lack of something to do and absence of interest, or, in other words, emptiness. I sometimes enjoy the art of doing nothing. At such times, I think about my life and consider if I'm on course as to where I want to sail. I can also sit in a chair by our tent camp and enjoy the countless beauties of the day or night."

"I enjoy your company the more I get of it," observed Jake.

"I'm starting to see this project coming to a conclusion and I'm regretting the loss of something I and the crew have so much enjoyed," explained Will. "That's why I'm talking more about our view of your home. Your home is beautiful, Jake Sands. And the cabin, along with lane, we are building are both good too. All I'm trying to say is we are pleased to have met you, the Sands Lodge and this wilderness."

"I've greatly enjoyed your company," repeated Jake. "I'll miss you when your project has been completed but we will all have a wonderful memory of this time."

"Thanks Jake," proclaimed Will. "That makes me feel better. We won't really leave because we'll have the memory."

"That's why a person's life itself is not in vain because there is the memory," mused Jake. "If, on earth, there is left only the record of a mound of shells, that is not where the real records are kept. The only important part of life—lasting aspect—is spiritual. Records are kept in the spiritual side, or as people sometimes call, heaven."

"I like listening to you Jake," said Will.

"I should add that I also sometimes enjoy the art of doing nothing," noted Jake. "Occasionally I'll sit out here, watch the wilderness of sea or land and just rest with them. There's nothing more peaceful than the sound of a forest or ocean on a beautiful day."

"Thanks for a great visit—wonderful project—Jake but I should get back to work," noted Will, before he stood.

"Thank you for good memories," added Jake, as the foreman turned and started walking back to his camp.

Jake gathered his fishing equipment and walked to the water's edge. Almost immediately, the great blue heron arrived. Outstretched wings neatly folded back along sleek sides, just as a snowy egret dropped from the sky, as if fishing could not occur unless all three fishermen were present.

Jake threw out the cast net. Lead weights on outer edges spread the net into a fully outstretched circle to splash onto the surface then drop below the water, just before Jake pulled on the line, closing the weights and enfolding any passing small fish or minnow. Jake shook the mesh over sand, releasing from the folds mullet and greenbacks. Most of the mullet went to the heron until this majestic hunter, actually full, spread its wings and climbed the sky, likely to watch the rest of the action from a recently acquired favorite place on the now completed roof of the cabin. The egret, full of minnows soon followed the other fisherman, leaving Jake to consider the fish he would pursue.

Having taken care of the present requirements of the other two fishermen—something that rarely happens, reasoned Jake, *maybe I'll try something different.* He put the remaining mullet into the bucket then dragged the boat to the water. He stepped inside, loaded his other equipment and rowed out to a weedy and shallow section of water along an adjacent stretch of shore. Using a mullet for bait, he dropped this line overboard then rowed away a suitable distance to see if any silver kings, or tarpon, might be in the area.

While he waited, a pelican dropped down to also wait at the back of the boat. This fisherman was pleased to be tossed some extra mullet. The fish entered the open beak then the fisherman, satisfied, stretched its wings and returned to patrol with other pelicans.

The next visitor was a vast cloud. It arrived from the west, was soon overhead and brought murkiness to the day before dropping rain in such a deluge it sprayed as a white sheet around the small boat. There was water everywhere. Saving an extra mullet for bait, Jake used the bucket to bail out his craft.

As quickly as the deluge had started, it moved away leaving in its path freshness of a renewed day. Something hit the bait, bending the pole. Jake waited, knowing that a tarpon would slam potential food with a tail hit before turning to feed.

Following a short wait, the pole bent into a half circle and the boat started moving. *Maybe I have a large silver fish on and this will be an interesting journey,* noted Jake. The fish pulled, the boat followed and Jake became impatient. He pulled on the line. In response, the surface ahead of the boat splashed upward around the rising form of an unbelievably large silver fish. Showing its agility, it turned in the air and reentered the water to start struggling more frantically than before. Again Jake pulled on the line. The large fish shot again from the surface in an accompanying circle of spray. Sunlight flashed along silver sides just before the hook was tossed skyward and the battle was won this time by the fish.

There are no fillets but lots of action, concluded Jake, before he started rowing back to camp. He got some frozen shrimp from his fridge, baited a line and sent it out where a slight breeze was starting to form waves. He sat on a comfortable chair and waited. The two birds, although once full, arrived and joined in the waiting routine, as if the search was just part of life. In reality, eating was only an aspect of the more important journey of seeking. They both, especially the great blue heron, watched the pole with its outstretched line.

To thank the birds for such interesting company, Jake used the net again to catch some greenback snacks. The watchers enjoyed the snacks then the waiting continued.

"Sands Lodge is for you too," said Jake, to his companions. Time passed, marked by the sun. When it was starting to drop toward the horizon, something pulled sharply on the line. Displaying vigorous fighting, a vertically striped sheepshead came to shore.

With one fish in the bucket and a crew to feed, Jake sent out the line again and almost immediately there was a second sheepshead added to the crew's fish fry. Jake kept sending out the baited line, catching fish until the action suddenly stopped because the school must have moved away. Stretching their wings then composing themselves again, as if to release some tension, the other two fishermen saw that action had concluded. They climbed the sky to end this day's fishing.

Jake carried his catch up to a table he had placed behind the tents and started filleting. He saved fillets for his evening's meal then took the rest to George.

Seeing the fillets arrive, George exclaimed, "Just when I think this place couldn't get any better or more interesting you prove maybe good things here have no end. Those fillets are really going to be special. There will be a fish fry tonight. What type of fish is on the menu today?"

"Sheepshead," answered Jake. "They are part of the perch family and, same as perch, a delicacy."

"Thanks Jake," said George. "Will you join us for a perch-relative meal?"

"Soon but not tonight," replied Jake. "Your invitations are appreciated."

"I just cook the stuff you bring in and the meals are the most varied and tasty the crew has ever had," said George. "They're starting to think I'm a good cook."

"Everyone knows that," added Jake, smiling, before he turned to walk back to his tent. Considering the day's action, I'm tired, he concluded. I think I'll fry fish and relax this evening.

Jake was cooking fillets when rain returned to pound against the tent's sides. The accompanying onrush of water seemed a natural accompaniment to a meal from the water. The pieces of fish, cooked to golden color and topped by malt vinegar, provided a best possible meal for the end of the day. Afterward, he cleaned the cooking area and sat down to listen to the tapping of diminishing rain against tent sides. He prepared a margarita from remnants Cindy had left.

The Sands Resort—or Lodge—is really a special place, he reflected. *It was rain that started a journey to this conclusion and maybe now I'll always welcome rain as a guidepost in my life. A wet day gave me time to search or tidy—explore—my attic and that activity brought me to the photograph of my great grandparents, Jessica and Feston Sands, standing at the back of Sands Lodge. Caught by that photo, I searched for the site where it had taken place and as a result came here. That photo brought me to this place where I feel more at home than I ever have. That photo was not of other people. It was a picture of my life—a self-portrait. I like the rain. It brought me here.*

Sleep came easily to Jake, accompanied by the muted splash of waves along the shore and a slight tapping of water dropping from palms and hitting the tent. A fresh breeze moved air with its slight fragrance of salt.

The next morning, first rays of sunlight shone on the world surrounding the cabin site making it fresh with the promise of a new beginning. Having finished breakfast, Jake enjoyed the scent of earth awakened by rain and adding vegetal traces to the air. *The area has been washed*, he observed, *and I think I'll try something to match the earth's freshness. I'll leave my house and visit my home.*

After placing a thermos of coffee and a cup in a backpack, he carried a folding chair then walked to the small rowboat the builders had built as an addition to the cabin. The craft was used to cross the inlet.

Jake rowed to the opposite shore then started walking along the trail. When he reached an area of massive live oaks, draped with moss, he left the trail, entered the wilderness and eventually sat on the chair in an opening surrounded by oaks where the wildness rang with calls of cardinals.

When I got lost, he recounted, *I received a vision showing me I was not alone and defeated but part of all my surroundings, where each life was connected to the spiritual, the connection being the Creator. I will return now to seek again a revelation.*

From the thermos, Jake filled the cup, sat back in the chair and waited. He observed all of the surrounding wildness where branches of live oaks covered much of the blue sky. Streamers of moss completed a stately atmosphere formed by towering trees. Cardinals put into song the physical beauty of wilderness.

Jake waited for a long period yet nothing happened. He returned the next day then every day for a week without results. He was starting to expect to see only physical outlines of wilderness when the area filled with light and seemed to jump toward him, making the oneness of everything more obvious. He saw his cabin in a vast, wild area just as it was approached by a small flock of doves. They flew under and beside one of the birds impeded by an injured wing. When the injured dove came to the region of the cabin, the broken wing was healed. After this healing, all members of the flock flew away in celebration with each dove using healthy wings.

Thinking about what he had seen, Jake walked back to the small boat, rowed it to the opposite shore and returned to his tent site. He went fishing with the company of heron and egret.

The birds showed little interest in a manatee passing just under the surface next to shore. Farther out, a turtle gulped air before slipping again below small waves. Dolphins also surfaced regularly to get air, while continuing a hunt for food. Pelicans, masters of fishing, with little effort soared above the water.

For the heron and egret, Jake threw out the net and brought in scaled sardines, or greenbacks, along with mullet. While his two companions were eating there was a sharp strike on the line and Jake brought in a king mackerel.

As the three fishermen continued to watch the bountiful sea, the sun moved lower, entered a red haze then gradually sank into it and gathered color and light before vanishing from view. As part of natural events with the sea's constant motion, the birds knew the time had come and they flew back into the sky to often reappear on top of the new cabin. They would be ready to go fishing again with the first light of dawn.

Jake walked to his tent, did the filleting and soon had fillets sending a tantalizing aroma into the salty air. Topped with malt vinegar, the meat was white and delicious. He followed the meal with tea.

Hooting of a great horned owl spoke to darkness before only rustling palm fronds, or leaves, gave sound to the night. A slight breeze laced with sea fragrances along with flowers filled the tent where Jake drifted into a deep sleep.

Fully refreshed in the morning, he, after breakfast, left his tent camp and walked to the water's edge where he started following the trail of sand between the wildness of the Gulf and wilderness of the land. A salty breeze seemed to be a connecting link between the two regions now in complete harmony.

Jake enjoyed the song of wind and waves as he rushed onward at top speed. He walked on, while the sun climbed higher, bringing more golden light and warmth.

This journey continued until he passed a restaurant followed by another, passing several resorts. In front of one resort, where he had rented a room, a person sat on a chair, fishing. Coming closer, Jake was pleased to recognize Tessa Taber.

When he approached her, she said, "You should have come sooner."

"I didn't know I was expected," he replied.

"You should've known," she said.

"I probably won't know what I'm not told," he countered.

"You are here now," she added, smiling brightly. "Could I get you a chair?"

"It's maybe too early," he answered, "but could I get you—treat you—to a restaurant of your choice?"

"Let's put this stuff away and go for a walk along the beach," she said.

Jake helped her carry equipment to her apartment above the clinic. Afterward, they returned to the beach.

"The restaurant is back the way you walked," she explained before they both proceeded to follow the edge of rushing water as each wave splashed then swirled up to a line in the sand. Sandpipers, as usual scurried in search of coquinas.

Florida

For Jake, the feeling of all things being in harmony filled him with increased energy and he could have walked a long way farther but Tessa turned and followed a path to a restaurant. The doors had just opened and remained that way allowing the salty breeze to enter. Tess selected a table at the far end of a wide room where open, screened windows presented a panorama of the Gulf.

"Good choice of restaurant," noted Jake.

"I don't come here often," she replied, "but I think it's the best place. It catches the atmosphere of beach and water. We are still outside even though we have entered a building."

"Anything for starters?" asked a woman who had arrived unnoticed and just finished fitting a freshly cleaned apron. She had dark hair and eyes along with being well tanned and seemed to carry herself with an attitude of one fully experienced in restaurant life. "I'm Ruby."

"I'm Tessa—or Tess," she replied, "And over here in the boxer trunks we have Jake."

Laughing, Ruby said, "Boxer trunks—now that's essential information. I insist on knowing that before getting your drink orders."

"A margarita," said Tess.

"And the same," added Jake.

"You're having a margarita?" asked Tess, after Ruby had walked to the bar.

"I'm celebrating," he answered.

"What are you celebrating?" she asked.

"Today," he explained.

"Wouldn't life be great if we could do that every day?" she mused, just as the drinks arrived.

"Thanks Ruby," said Jake while she placed menus on the table.

"Some days have a special harmony to them," he added. They fill you with overflowing energy because there are no side issues draining strength. With extra support. there's also a feeling of optimism, thinking there is smooth sailing ahead and an ability to keep above the storms. Today I met you."

"I hoped you would arrive sooner," she continued.

"As I mentioned before, I didn't know," he explained.

"I listened to you," said Tessa. "You talk about the wilderness and I wanted to live in the world you described.

How could I contribute, I wondered? Then I knew. I have used my influence to add to the veterinary clinic, a wildlife rescue center for all wildlife—birds and animals. We'll heal them so they can rejoin their wilderness lives."

"Wonderful news," exclaimed Jake. He took an extra amount of the drink, slowly put down the glass, looked out at the Gulf and, almost whispering, said, "I saw this coming. Sometimes life is only a storm and the sky is so dark we are shielded from just how bad the situation is. Then there are days, such as those recent and today, when events flow with such an apparent, even noticeable, sacred effect. We must question why we can't see such powerful good in life at the worst of times. What I'm trying to say is, I saw the healing of wildlife coming. Wild creatures would come to the wilderness of the cabin, get healed then return to the joy of their wild lives."

"You wandered away, Jake," observed Tess. "Are you back?"

"Never left," he confirmed. "I'm just pleased to hear about the wildlife rescue clinic."

"With all that's happening," she continued, "an accountant is needed to keep order. You were highly recommended, if you want the job."

"Wonderful news," he exclaimed. "Of course I want to be part of such a project."

"Ready to order?" asked Ruby who had approached again, unnoticed.

"Two grouper sandwiches with cheese," replied Tess.

"That's our favorite—always requested meal," noted Ruby. "Cheese is usually not mentioned. Another round?"

"Yes," answered Tess.

"You are a lady of surprises," said Jake. "Thank you for ordering the grouper sandwiches—with cheese. You are in the harmony of my day."

"I saw that when I met you," she replied.

"I think I saw that with you although I thought I was only dreaming," recalled Jake.

"Sometimes they come true," she said. "I saw the same."

The sandwiches arrived along with other drinks. "Thanks Ruby," said Tess before Ruby left and the meal started.

While each one gathered the surroundings of breezes entering screens along with the added presence of the Gulf to enjoyment of food, time passed.

After they returned to sipping margaritas, Jake said, "My cabin and lane are almost finished. Some days when you are out for walks or drives you should visit."

As Jake had done previously, Tessa took some extra time to gather the surroundings of breezes through screens and panorama of the Gulf where waves crashed along a sandy shoreline, before she said, "In all ways you are unique, Jake. On other waterfront properties, people have mansions."

"I have a mansion," he countered.

"A cabin—a lane?" she asked.

"The wilderness around the cabin and lane is the mansion," he explained.

"There's nothing other people have built to compare."

"Seeing that is what most people miss—at their peril," stated Tess. "These margaritas are fine but I know where they are better."

"Oh," he exclaimed. "Maybe we should go there."

"Nothing people have built can compare," she added, smiling beautifully.

"If more days were like this then life would be too easy," he said, while placing cash on the table. "All we would have to do, sitting back is watch harmony take place where each part comes together and we would hear the ring of events merging in a golden glow of resulting light and we could see the spirit in the midst of life."

"Ready?" she asked, standing.

"A long time ago," he replied.

They left the building and Tessa said, "I have some things to get and I could meet you down at the dunes."

"OK," he replied before they started walking in different directions.

She met him later and pulled two glasses out of a paper bag. From a second container, she removed a bottle of margarita then filled the two glasses, before giving one to Jake.

"You're right," he said. "This is the best restaurant I've ever seen."

They sipped the drinks slowly while discussing their lives from the past to the present and some of the future. The day moved past with all parts continuing as in measureless time. Colors of sunset filled the sky and topped the Gulf's surface.

Gradually the sinking sun retrieved color and light, bringing on night's realm. Slowly the scene changed until a path of silver light spread across the Gulf from the moon to shore where the two people left their clothes on a slanting edge of dune then the best of times for them started.

In the morning, when the sun returned light to sea and land, the warming rays touched Tessa while she returned to her apartment and clinic. Jake walked home to check on the progress of finalizing the building of the lane and cabin.

Back at his tent camp, he slept much of the time until he started early the next morning to enjoy breakfast. Following cups of coffee, he met his two friends at the water's edge where they were greeted by an approaching cloud of screaming gulls. The scramble was a moving feast with birds attacking minnows as they jumped from the surface to avoid fish striking from below.

Waiting for a clear spot, Jake threw out the net. When he pulled it back to shore, there was, in the trap, a large catch of jacks along with scaled sardines. The heron and egret quickly picked out most minnows, although Jake saved some for bait. He also filled much of the bucket with jacks.

The mass of life moved farther along the shoreline and gradually out of view. Jake tried baiting his line with a shrimp as a change of selection for a passing fish.

So much had happened so early that the sea withheld its supply and nothing moved the line. Seeing some mullet in the water, Jake threw out the net, catching enough to fill the heron. The egret received some greenbacks from the bait supply.

Fish stopped biting. *While the water rests*, thought Jake, *I have time to focus on this area. I enjoy the company of the birds. We are a team. They have all the skills to catch food in their own ways. These hunters also know the catches are greater if we fish together rather than separately and, maybe too, they enjoy company. Their lives are linked with other parts of life as I discovered more clearly when I got lost in the wilderness. I too am connected yet I so often fail to understand the position of others. I thought Cindy would stay although she had no such intentions. She was here to have a holiday away from her life as it was going to be. I thought her holiday was her life and soon discovered my mistake. Now I see a tie with Tessa. I wonder what she sees. I've learned my view is not always the same as that perceived by another person—or anyone. Along this shore, people build mansions of mortar and brick. I, as the Seminoles saw the mansion was the wilderness. Nothing people could build was, in any way, a match for the splendor already present. The cabin was not the home but just a place to stay and cook meals, sleep or rest. Anything I would build here reduces the value of the property as others along this shore, with brick and mortar, have impoverished their own lives. We misinterpret and thereby destroy the environment at our own peril. Greater storms are starting to indicate to all people that true progress does not include destruction of the sky, land or sea. Will and George, along with the others, may wonder why I have shown such little interest in the work being done at the cabin and lane. My interest is with my home and not for the shelter, providing a place to visit my house.*

The sea never rests even when it seems calm, observed Jake. *Most aspects of wilderness are the same. The heron and egret, at times seem to be as still as statues but their eyes are always alert and watching.*

The breeze moved small waves to shore where they splashed along the border of sand. Clouds drifted slowly past the sun as if to show time passing. A moment, after passing could never be recalled or stopped from fading. *Time, a moment—a day,* thought Jake *should never be wasted because, at its completion, can never be recalled.*

Can't slow life down either, observed Jake. *I must make the best of it. Only spiritual life lasts forever. There we should store our accomplishments. My mansion will last while the brick and mortar mansions along this shore will be left behind, when the owners leave.*

A slam on the line startled all three fishermen. The pole bent. Egret and heron stretched wings, getting ready for action. The thrusts on the line were steady and not sharp and unpredictable as those of a shark or mackerel. Following a steady battle, Jake pulled to shore a large snook. Working quickly, he baited the line again with shrimp, sending out this attraction and brought to shore another snook followed by a sheepshead. As a change, he tried a scaled sardine for bait and almost immediately brought in a mackerel. He gave much of the remaining minnows to the other two fishermen. After filling their stomaches, they stretched out wings and returned to the sky and moved out of view to likely appear again at the tent camp or on the cabin's roof.

Jake took his catch to George. With the pail almost empty again, it was ready for the next day's catch.

"I've saved one snook for tonight's meal," said Jake to the cook, who was always happy to get fresh food. "I also have some mullet and minnows for the birds to enjoy the next day."

"The crew has never eaten so well," exclaimed George. "Thanks for the fish. I've another hog for the spit."

After checking the new supply of fish, George looked around at the Gulf and surrounding landscape and said, "All of us on the crew enjoy our work. This is our occupation. Your project though has been different from the others. There's something about this area that's special. We all know we are working but we also have a feeling of being on holiday. That's our mood—or spirit—as we go about so-called working. There's a presence here. Maybe the difference with this site is the fact the wilderness prevails and the buildings are minimal. That's it. That's the difference. We are in the wilderness of the land and sea."

"You have noticed what this place is," stated Jake. "My home is the wilderness and not the cabin."

"You have explained what we have all been experiencing," observed the happy cook.

"Fishing was good today," added Jake. "We'll see what the Gulf has for us tomorrow."

Back at his tent, Jake had more filleting to do then frying added tantalizing fragrances to the salty breeze. Snook provided delicious, white meat and was accompanied by a slice of pork from the meat George had contributed.

I've always wanted to supply the crew with fish, noted Jake, while he sipped beer as he sat and watched afternoon colors and sounds of his surroundings. *I only catch as much fish as people need—and never more. I just fish for needed food. One time, I talked to a hunter who explained how he and other hunters used the meat of animals killed during the hunting trip. By trying to justify the killing, he exposed the tragedy. The meat was not needed, but just used after the animal was shot.*

The fish supply will vary, observed Jake, again after obtaining another can of beer. *There will be days when waves will be too high or storms will hit the region. I won't always find one day after another to be suitable for fishing.*

As Tessa said, he recalled, *most people along the waterfront build great mansions. These places are of brick and mortar, while my estate is the surrounding wilderness, including land and sea. My home is alive, which makes all the difference.*

The next day brought strong wind. It shook the tent and became an accompanying whirring sound while Jake prepared breakfast. Afterward, Jake walked to the water's edge. Large waves stood up in walls of water. They crested before crashing on the shore, sending turbulent sheets of water, spreading forward then rushing back to be replaced by the next flow. Beside this activity, Jake walked. *I enjoy such action*, he reflected while proceeding onward at a fast pace. *At such times, I see the strength of wind and hear the power of the Gulf as it sends great waves to shore.* Occasionally, sunlight broke from clouds and shone into walls of cresting waves. In one brightened expanse of rising water, a school of fish swam by. *Likely mullet*, thought Jake.

Although the water and wind caught most of his attention, he also scanned the sand, particularly after it was swept by a passing flow. Seeing an intriguing object rising amid turbulence, he rushed forward, dislodged the mystery and exclaimed to himself, *pottery—part of a bowl and likely made by the Timucuans who, as me, called this place home.*

Seeing other intriguing objects lying on the sand, he hurried to investigate, finding some of them to be special shark teeth. *These are of medium, almost large size,* he noted. *They are also lighter in color than most teeth.*

Seeing numerous teeth farther out from shore, Jake scrambled to get them before the next wave hit. He gathered up most of them and was turning to escape the water when behind him he heard a rushing sound just before there was a crash. He was tumbled into a turbulent mixture of sand and water then dropped on the beach at the end of a flow. He dug in his heels to resist the backflow but it took him into the base of the next wave. Again he was deposited up on sand where he managed to roll out of the returning onrush of water.

I have saved some treasures from the fascinating sea, he mused while he checked the teeth he had managed to save. *I'll tie wire harnesses on them and make pendants.*

Jake was making pendants in his tent when George arrived bringing another slab of roasted pork. "There's much more if you want it," said the cook.

"Thank you," replied Jake. "Did this fellow get shot?"

"Yes," he answered. "He was snared first. Just didn't have a good day at all."

"You must be the world's most popular cook," observed Jake.

"You've been making me look good," he said.

George returned to his work at the main camp, while Jake prepared a meal using the most recent acquired pork. Will arrived bringing beer. Both men sat in chairs in front of the tents. Watching the Gulf send waves to shore, while palms bent in the wind, Will reported, "You will soon be viewing the restless Gulf from the comforts of your cabin, while your car is parked at the back."

"You are an extraordinary group of workers," observed Jake. "As you, I don't wear ornaments of any kind but I have an exception to this custom." As he spoke, he brought out some of the pendants, and explained, "I went for a walk along the beach while waves were sweeping across the sand and found some treasures from the sea. I've made pendants from them and have one each for you, George and the rest of the crew."

Receiving the teeth, Will said, "You know, that's something I'm going to wear," and he put one around his neck. "Thanks Jake. This has been a special time in a place as no other I've ever been; and here I've picked up from this shore a piece of information. This tooth reminds me that nothing on earth lasts forever, except the spiritual world. That's what you've told me and this tooth I will wear as a reminder of that advice and this special time."

Will rushed back to his camp and distributed the pendants in which he had taken a special interest. He added the message that came with each tooth. The workers all wore a shark tooth.

Will returned to Jake's camp and carried two paper plates. Each one was topped with a celebration sandwich.

After the meal, a beer routine continued and Will reported, "The men are really pleased with the pendants. The teeth are timely gifts because our work here is coming to an end. I feel as if I'm reaching the last days of a holiday."

"I'm going to miss the company," said Jake. "Of course, I hope you will visit the Sands Lodge."

"Yes," replied Will.

"There are days for me, and likely for you, when no light shines through the darkness and even hope cannot be seen," stated Jake.

"Yes," said Will. "I don't think those days visit the Sands Lodge."

"That's when you have to have faith, even though in the dark days that's hard to do," continued Jake. "The sea taught me today, there is danger present, such as getting too close to tall waves but there are the best of times and treasure to be won all the time. Today the sea showed me potential danger along with grand and great treasures to be discovered. Through all of these experiences, there arrive occasions, such as now, when all the pieces of life can be seen as fitting together in harmony showing us, as lighthouses or buoys along the way, we our following along our true journeys, with success."

"When you gave me the pendant and I distributed the others," replied Will, "I was thinking the way you have been talking. You have put into words, the way I saw the men react to their treasures."

The next morning, after breakfast, Jake had a feeling of being caught up in momentum and joy of life when it is in harmony with all parts fitting together, as pieces of a puzzle. Will arrived, saying, "Would you come for a walk?"

Jake followed Will to the laneway where the foreman stopped and said, "You can now bring your car to your cabin. The lane is finished."

"It's just as I hoped—and knew—you would do it," observed Jake. "Nothing has been disturbed of the landscape other than to expand the path to allow a car to use the trail."

"Would you care to go for another walk?" asked the foreman.

"Your walks are very interesting," replied Jake, before he started to follow again and soon they were at the cabin. "Your cabin is finished," announced Will. "You can move in. Hopefully it is just as you have requested."

While the two men looked over the structure, Will said, "We, of course entered the south side into the kitchen area then we step into the one main room where there is a wood fireplace along with woodstove and gas—propane—fireplace and air conditioner. This is a small place but really has everything. There's, of course, the washroom, other door, two back bedrooms and one up in the loft."

"Perfect," exclaimed Jake. "As the lane, this is everything I hoped for and was confident to see."

"You checked the building sites less than any person we've ever worked with in the past," said Will.

"I was interested, of course," replied Jake. "I was confident with the building and carried on with life at the tents, enjoying the surrounding landscape and Gulf."

"We are starting to fold up the work place," said Will. "We all feel a holiday has ended at the Sands Lodge."

"If all people leaving disturbs me as much as you and your crew finishing, I don't think I would enjoy running an actual lodge," observed Jake. "If that day returns, I'll contact you."

"I'll tell the men," exclaimed Will. "We have something to look forward to."

Will walked away and action at camp continued with the removal of structures and loading of boats. Jake was also busy moving into his new cabin.

With all work complete, he awakened for the first morning in the loft of the cabin. Looking up in the first light of dawn, he could just distinguish the ceiling boards. They filled the air with a slight fragrance of pine. Moving down the steps, he prepared breakfast in the compact kitchen. He made coffee with water coming in from the well at the back. A power line running next to the lane brought in electricity. An outside propane tank fueled the gas fireplace, if it was needed.

After breakfast, Jake sat in what he knew would be his favorite chair next to the woodstove and gas fireplace, facing the two front windows on each side of the wood fireplace. Through these windows, the Gulf could always be seen by anyone in the room. All other windows revealed the presence of surrounding wilderness of the land.

Jake sipped coffee and, through the front windows, watched the Gulf. *A long time ago, a rainy day kept me inside my house up north and, having extra time, I checked the attic and looked into some old records*, he recalled. There I found a photograph of Jessica and Feston Sands, *my great grandparents, standing in front of Sands Lodge. Now I'm there—at the site of the lodge. Their world is now mine. Am I living my own life or just following theirs? I can answer that question because I'm not trying to copy anyone. My journey, in my own way, has brought me to the same home Jessica, Feston, and others have also enjoyed. The place is similar, while each life is unique—as each person makes different choice even when walking along the same route. This cabin is perfect. It provides a sheltered camp where I can enjoy my home. My car is parked outside at the back. The crew left the small rowboat for crossing the inlet to get to the trail leading to Roger Tomkins' cabin. There is also the boat and motor at the front beach.*

Above the back door, Jake placed a sign similar to the one he had seen in the photo he found in the attic. This sign stated Sands Lodge. While adding this finishing project, Jake noticed the egret and heron had returned to their places on the ridge of the cabin roof. These locations had become their territories. The birds could be found on the ridge through much of a day from dawn until dusk. Jake saved minnows for the egret and other small fish such as mullet for the heron. The birds were fed when they appeared at first light of dawn. Sometimes these sentinels could be seen on the roof at night.

With a sign above the back door as in the photo and birds claiming their positions on the cabin's roof, everything has been completed with the cabin, observed Jake, while he sat in a favorite chair next to the gas fireplace and sipped the second cup of coffee for the day.

Maybe today is the first routine time at the new Sands Lodge.

When he carried his fishing equipment and walked to the beach, the heron and egret left their places on the cabin's ridge and met him at the water's edge. Jake threw out the cast net and brought back a good supply of scaled sardines or greenbacks. A second toss brought in some mullet. With this supply, he filled the bait bucket and fed the birds.

After baiting the hook, Jake sent the line out as far as possible then the three fishermen waited. Each one watched the pole and line. Excitement started when the line went taut and the pole bent. The first action brought to shore a slender ladyfish and this went to the heron. To not leave out the smaller fisherman, Jake tossed the egret some minnows from the bucket.

As the sun left red and pink mist in the east during a gradual rise to mark the time of morning leading to noon, the morning gathered to itself many of the aspects of a perfect day by the sea. A slight salty breeze sent small waves to splash along the shore where sandpipers waited to search for coquinas. Pelicans soared past, resuming their patrols for fish. At seemingly routine times of day, the dolphins broke from the surface while they swam past, following the shore. More unusual was Jake seeing a turtle, as it surfaced to get air. A manatee moved along near the shore, causing only a slight ripple at the surface.

The sun gradually moved past the middle point before beginning a descent into afternoon when the pole bent, the three fishermen braced for action and Jake brought to shore a Spanish mackerel. A second mackerel came in shortly afterward then a third. Jake threw out the net to add to the birds' food not just for this trip but also during their meals at the first light of each day.

The three fishermen went to the cabin. The two birds received extra treats while Jake filleted mackerel behind the cabin. Afterward, Jake took fillets inside while the two birds rested on the ridge of the roof. From there, they watched the world of land and sea. They also watched for Jake and did not miss any fishing trips.

Florida

He was dusting fillets with corn meal to prepare a meal when he heard a car stop at the back of the cabin. *A first visitor*, he noted before turning off the stove and walking to the back door. Opening it, he was pleased to see Tessa Taber.

She wore a red, corduroy cap over her blonde hair and her eyes seemed to be of a lighter blue than usual when she flashed a lovely smile and said, "Hi Jake. I like your cabin. Do you know you have two birds on the roof?"

"Yes," he answered. "They live here—and you are a welcome sight at the Sands Lodge."

"Thank you," she replied, stepping inside. "I noticed your sign and the interior has everything needed without extras to get in the way of enjoying the natural world we are all here to see."

"You have a great and accurate impression of the place," he added. "What could I get for you?"

"Nothing now," she replied. "Maybe I'll just sit down and enjoy this place."

She sat on a sofa along the north wall. From there she could watch the cabin plus see outside to the land and Gulf. "Being in here is the same as sitting outside," she declared.

"That's what this cabin is," agreed Jake. "It provides a full view of my living mansion—the land and sea."

"At the wildlife refuge we are ready to have you start working as the accountant," explained Tess. "More than accounting, they also want you to help look after birds and animals to get them back to health so they can be released again to the natural world and their natural lives."

"I will like caring for wildlife even more than accounting," exclaimed Jake.

"I told them you would enjoy helping to heal wildlife," she said. "You can use the egret and heron on your roof as references."

"I'm sure they'd put in a good word for me," he added, laughing. "Three of us live here—not just one."

"That's the whole beauty of this realm of the Sands Lodge," exclaimed Tess, beaming. "The cabin is part of the wild while you work at the refuge to help heal birds and animals. We are not only linked to the wilderness but we are healing it—and maintaining the most beautiful part of life."

"Speaking of beauty of life, I hope you will be part of this cabin," said Jake as he prepared more fillets then turned on the stove.

"I sort of am already," she said. "I'm visiting to mention they want you to start at the refuge."

"I discussed this with the egret and heron," said Jake. "They agreed that this cabin world could include—already does include—one more."

"Thanks Jake," she said, "and I'll thank the birds on the way out."

Leaving the small kitchen, Jake walked toward Tess and, giving her a shark tooth pendant, said, "This is part of your membership."

"Oh, thanks Jake," she said, placing the leather cord around her head and letting the tooth settle into place. "Superb shark tooth."

"They washed up during a storm," he explained. "They are a sign of special membership here at the Sands Lodge and also a reminder that nothing lasts forever, except the spiritual world. The wilderness is a messenger of the spirit."

"There's a lot hanging around my neck," she said, smiling and flashing a glance of beauty that caused Jake to turn off the stove.

"Maybe we should have a margarita first," he offered.

"OK," she replied before leaving the building. From the trunk of her car she removed some packages and carried them back inside the cabin. "I'll have a margarita mixed in a moment."

Working quickly, she soon had two colorful glasses prepared. She gave one to Jake, who sat in his favorite chair next to the fireplace, as Tess returned to the sofa.

"I came prepared, Jake," she said. "You don't have a chance."

They both sipped from the drinks and they added to a mood of celebration when Tess said, "Have another long sip Jake. You are going to need it because if I waited for you, I might as well watch a tree grow. One would take just as long as the other."

"Not sure I know what you're getting at here," said Jake, "but you are sending out the bait and if you are fishing I don't mind being the fish."

Florida

"You have to be the fish because I'm too impatient to be the recipient," she said.

"This is all a mystery to me," he said, "as much of a certain world is" said Jake.

"So it's a good thing you met me," added Tess.

"Getting downright confusing," he confessed. "I'm out of my territory."

"Time to set the hook," she said. "Have another sip."

"OK," he said. "At least that's back to something I understand."

He enjoyed an extra amount of margarita, lowered his glass and Tess, with a pale light in her eyes, said, "Jake I was thinking with your cabin finished, your life now established as part of the wilderness, and we are healing wildlife at the refuge, the time is right for the natural step that really has happened already, although you haven't noticed that time has come for you and I to get married."

"Wow," he said. "And I thought fishing was exciting."

"This is fishing," she said, laughing. "I am just far too impatient to wait for you to set the hook. So, are you caught or not."

"I was caught a long time ago," he declared. "I just didn't know what to do about it."

"That's why I went fishing," she said. "I knew what to do."

"If we all do our best the world is better place," he mused. "You are my first visitor and hopefully you won't leave."

"Thanks Jake," she said. "Most of my stuff is in the car."

"I thought I understood the world," he mused, "but there's so much of it I don't grasp."

"That's why two people often work together," she said. "You and those birds work together, each one enriches the other. The wilderness is so important for us to keep as part of our lives—an essential spirit. Wildlife is also much of our lives. The tragedy of our times is the loss of wilderness. Our role is to help heal it."

They unloaded the car then Jake served the meal. "You're a good cook, Jake," said Tess, while they savored the fried mackerel dinner.

"We are dining on fish now," he noted. "The birds have filled up on fish this morning. So much of the world depends on fish and they need clean water and a natural environment."

"At the refuge," noted Tess, "we focus on healing birds and animals. We also have a promotional section about the importance of fish and the sea. That is part of the world you have here. You have maintained the wilderness of the land and sea. Each is essential and from your cabin we live with these outer mansions."

"This is your first meal at the lodge," said Jake. "For the next occasion, I'm going to make for you something I learned from Roger Tomkins and that's a celebration sandwich."

"It isn't just your sandwich that is a celebration," she said. "That speaks of our time here. We have not shut out or left outside but have made part of this structure the spiritual realm. There's a transcending mood, a gathering together of all parts of the spiritual world. We could call this place the celebration lodge."

Following the meal, while the heron and egret watched from the ridge of the roof, Jake and Tessa, sipping margaritas, sat on chairs in front of the cabin and Jake said, "Some day in the future, a person will be looking through a portfolio of old pictures and will see a photo of you and I standing at the back of this cabin below its sign, Sands Lodge. On its roof, there will be an egret and a heron. The photo will hook the viewer and bring this person here to research and locate the story of Tessa and Jake Sands in a living mansion where natural land meets the wild sea."

ABOUT THE AUTHOR

Daniel Hance Page is a writer with over thirty books published and others being written. His books are authentic stories filled with action, adventure, history and travel including Native American traditions and spiritual insights to protect our environment in the smallest park or widest wilderness.

Made in the USA
Middletown, DE
19 November 2023